I0780644

Christmas Burns

Cynthia Hickey

The Sheriff of Misty Hollow, Book 6

Prologue

In the early morning hours right before dawn, he crouched in the cold and watched lights twinkle in a window. His hand trembled as he clutched the gasoline can. Not from fear, but from rage.

His sweet Lilly had died during the Christmas season last year. No one in Misty Hollow had cared. Life had gone on for the town's residents as if something sweet had not been taken from them.

"If I can't have Christmas, nobody can." He struck a match and tossed it through the window he'd shattered a few minutes before. Heat washed over his face as the Christmas tree ignited.

The flames erupted like a beast unchained. Red and gold light danced across the pristine snow, flickering against icicles hanging from the eaves. A plastic Santa melted on the front lawn, its cheerful face warping into something grotesque as the synthetic material bubbled and collapsed. The stench of burning plastic mingled with the sharp scent of pine needles being consumed.

He watched for only a few minutes before retreating into the woods. His breath curled in the air like small ghosts, dissipating into the darkness between the skeletal trees. Behind him, the house groaned and crackled as the fire spread through its bones.

It had been his fault. Lilly had died because he hadn't had the money to replace the old space heater. When it had sparked that December night, the tree had gone up in seconds. He'd been outside gathering firewood, arms full of frozen logs, when he heard her scream. By the time he dropped the wood and broke through the front door, flames were already licking at the ceiling. The smoke had been so thick, so black. He'd crawled on his hands and knees, calling her name until his voice was raw. But the fire had claimed her faster than love could save her.

Neighbors and the fire department had arrived muttering, "Tragedy. Poor child. Negligence!" Then nothing after the first few days. The sympathy had dried up like summer rain on hot pavement. No one had come to his aid. No one offered shelter, food, or a job. The insurance company had denied his claim, citing the faulty heater as negligence. The state had taken what remained of his property for back taxes he couldn't pay without work, without hope.

The funeral had been small. A handful of

townspeople attended out of obligation rather than grief. They whispered behind gloved hands about proper maintenance and parental responsibility. Not one of them had offered to help him bury his daughter. He'd dug the grave himself in the frozen cemetery ground, each shovelful of earth feeling heavier than the last.

He hid out in an abandoned cabin on the mountain, a relic from the old logging days. No power, no heat—only a rotting cot, a rusted stove, and memories that haunted every shadow. The cabin leaked when it rained and creaked in the wind like an old man's bones.

Nearby sat Lily's melted snow globe, the one with the tiny village inside where it was always Christmas morning. The glass had cracked from the heat of that terrible night, and the artificial snow had yellowed with age. Next to it lay a warped and silent music box, its ballerina frozen mid-dance, the melody trapped forever in twisted metal.

With a red crayon, he marked an X on the cracked wall above the stove. The waxy mark stood out like dried blood against the weathered wood.

One down.

The Hendersons had been first because they lived closest to his old home. They'd watched the flames that night from their warm living room, sipping hot cocoa while his world burned. Margaret Henderson had even complained to the fire chief about the smoke affecting her Christmas party. Their house had been easy—

colonial style with plenty of dry timber and a Christmas tree positioned perfectly near the front window.

But there were others. The Millers, who'd crossed the street rather than speak to him after the funeral. The Pattersons, who'd bought his property at auction for a fraction of its worth. Old Man Garrett, who'd fired him from the hardware store when customers started avoiding "that careless father." Each name was etched in his memory like headstones in a cemetery.

The second house would be different. He'd learned from the first. The gasoline needed to be spread more carefully, the escape route planned with precision. The Millers kept a spare key under their garden gnome—he'd watched them use it countless times when he still lived in the neighborhood, back when he was still part of their community.

Dawn was breaking now, painting the sky the color of embers. Smoke rose in a thin column from the valley below. Sirens wailed like banshees in the distance. Soon they would find the remains of the Henderson house, and Margaret would weep for her lost Christmas ornaments while her neighbors comforted her with casseroles and sympathy—the same kindness they'd never offered him.

He pulled his torn coat tighter against the morning chill. Tonight, when the town settled into false security, he would strike again. There would be more red X marks on his cabin wall before this Christmas season ended.

In his pocket, Lilly's small metal angel pressed against his fingers. It had been her favorite ornament, somehow surviving the fire that claimed everything else. The paint was chipped now, the wings blackened, but it remained. A reminder that some things endured, even when everything beautiful burned away.

The wind picked up, carrying the scent of smoke and the promise of snow. Winter was settling over Misty Hollow like a shroud, and with it came the longest nights of the year. Perfect weather for fires. Perfect weather for justice served cold and burning bright.

Two down, he would write tonight. Then three. Then four. Until the whole town understood what it meant to lose something precious, to watch helplessly as everything you loved turned to ash and memory.

Until Christmas died in Misty Hollow, just as it had died in him.

Chapter One

Shea Callahan stepped onto her front porch and did some stretching exercises in preparation for her morning jog. The late November air bit at her exposed skin as she worked through her routine—calf stretches against the porch railing, hamstring pulls, ankle rotations. When she straightened, she spotted the orange glow of flames in the valley below. Fire.

The glow painted the pre-dawn sky an ominous shade of amber, far too bright and too early to be anything innocent. Her stomach dropped with the familiar dread that came with emergencies in small towns—where everyone knew everyone, and tragedy touched them all.

She grabbed the truck keys from a hook inside the door. "Come, Heidi. We've got to go." The German Shepherd bounded from her bed by the fireplace, instantly alert. Seconds later, they sped down the mountain, Shea's truck navigating the winding road while Heidi pressed her nose against the passenger window.

Over her radio came the location of the fire. A home in the newly built community around the golf course. Whispering Pines Development, where city folks had built weekend retreats and retirement homes among the native pines and mountain laurel.

The radio crackled with updates from dispatch. "Structure fully involved. Fire department en route. No reports of occupants at this time." Shea pressed harder on the accelerator, her truck's headlights cutting through the lingering darkness as dawn struggled to break through the smoke-hazed horizon.

By the time she arrived, Deputy Trevor Bolton and the fire department had beaten her there. Fire trucks lined the narrow street like red sentinels, their emergency lights casting alternating waves of red and white. Firefighters worked methodically, their heavy coats steaming in the cold air as they directed streams of water onto what remained of the structure.

"Accident?" She studied the smoldering embers of what had once been a lovely two-story home. The colonial-style house had been one of the development's showcase properties, with its wrap-around porch and carefully manicured landscaping. Now, nothing more than a pile of blackened bricks and scorched timber remained. The chimney stood like a lone grave marker among the ruins.

"Arson." Trevor pointed to a gas can tossed into

the nearby bushes, the red plastic container stark against the snow-covered juniper shrubs. "The culprit had splashed gasoline across the lawn ornaments and inside the house. You can still smell it if you get close enough."

Shea approached the perimeter that Trevor had established with yellow tape. The acrid stench of burned synthetic materials mixed with gasoline fumes and the earthy smell of wet ash. A melted Santa decoration lay twisted on what had been the front lawn, its wire frame contorted into an abstract sculpture of destruction.

"Any of the neighbors see anything?" Shea glanced at the crowd gathered on the other side of the street. About twenty people stood in clusters, some wrapped in bathrobes and winter coats hastily thrown over pajamas. Steam rose from coffee mugs and the breath of hushed conversations.

"No. Everyone was asleep. Mrs. Potter said she noticed the fire when her poodle started barking around four-thirty." Trevor gestured toward an elderly woman clutching a small white dog. "She'd gotten out of bed, seen the flames through her bedroom window, and called the fire department. It was too late by the time they arrived. The structure was already compromised."

Fire Chief Bradford approached them, pulling off his helmet to reveal gray hair matted with sweat despite the cold. "Sheriff, we've got the fire contained, but there's not much left to save. Whoever did this knew what they were doing. They used an accelerant and targeted the areas that would cause maximum damage in minimum time."

"Professional job?"

"Maybe, or someone with experience. The burn pattern suggests they doused the Christmas tree first. That would have gone up like a torch and spread to the rest of the house quickly." Bradford wiped soot from his forehead. "We'll know more once our investigator gets here, but this was definitely intentional."

"Anyone home?"

Trevor shook his head. "The Miller family had spent the night at the wife's parents' home. Said they do it every Thanksgiving weekend. A kind of family tradition. They were planning to come back this morning to finish decorating for Christmas."

"Lucky for them." Shea watched as the firefighters continued their work, now more focused on preventing flare-ups than active suppression. "Not a great start to the holiday season."

She made her way to where the Miller family huddled under blankets in their blue minivan, their faces pale with shock and exhaustion. The vehicle's engine ran, heater blasting, but they still shivered. She tapped on the window, noting the Michigan license plates—transplants, like so many who'd discovered Misty Hollow in recent years.

"Any idea who would want to burn down your house?" She kept her voice gentle but direct.

"No, sheriff." Mr. Miller exited the van, closing the door behind him to keep the warmth in. He was a tall man in his forties, with the soft hands and pale complexion of someone who worked behind a desk. "We're new to Misty Hollow. Moved in a couple of months ago after this development was built. Bought the house as a new start. We don't know many people here yet."

"Any problems with contractors, neighbors, anyone who might have felt wronged?"

Miller shook his head, then paused. "Well, there was one thing. When we were moving in, an older man stopped by. Said he used to live somewhere around here, that his house had burned down. He seemed... off. Angry, maybe. But nothing threatening."

"Remember his name?"

"No, sorry. My wife might. She talked to him longer than I did." Miller glanced back at the van where a woman in her thirties sat with two young children. "She's pretty shaken up right now."

"That's understandable. We'll need to talk to her later, when she's feeling up to it." Shea handed him her card. "In the meantime, if you think of anything else, call me directly."

"It's a wonder none of the other houses caught fire," Miller said, looking at the neighboring homes that stood unscathed just thirty feet away.

"The snow helped." She again scanned the watching crowd. Was the arsonist there? Many enjoyed sticking around to watch the aftermath of their crime, feeding off the chaos and attention their actions had created. Her eyes moved from face to face, looking for anyone who seemed too interested, too eager, or oddly calm amid the destruction.

"Here." Trevor handed her a cup of coffee in a paper cup with the "Lucy's Diner" logo. "Lucy brought these from the diner. Said we could all use some."

"She's right." In times of crisis, Lucy often appeared like an angel of mercy with coffee and sandwiches for first responders. Shea wrapped her cold hands around the warm cup and breathed deeply of the rich aroma as she strolled across the street to question the gathered neighbors.

The crowd parted slightly as she approached, offering the deference small-town residents showed their sheriff. She recognized most of the faces. The Pattersons from the hardware store, old Mrs. Waterford who taught piano lessons, the Garrett brothers who ran the gas station.

"Remember the fire last year?" A woman mentioned to another. "The one where the little girl died?"

Shea paused, her attention sharpening. The woman speaking was Janet Reeves, who worked at the bank and knew everyone's business.

"Sure, I do. A real tragedy. That was an accident, though. Faulty heater." The second woman wrapped a quilt tighter around her shoulders. This was Beth

Thornton, who managed the post office and served as the town's unofficial news network.

"Maybe." Janet's tone held doubt.

"Mind telling me about that fire?" Shea asked, stepping closer to the two women.

"Well, it was Gary Richardson and his little girl, Lilly. She was maybe six or seven—sweetest child you ever saw." Janet's expression softened with remembered affection. "They lived in that old house on Elm Street, the one with the big oak tree in front. Gary was a handyman, did odd jobs around town. Never married Lilly's mother—she left town when the baby was small."

Beth picked up the story. "Last December, right before Christmas, a space heater sparked. The whole house burned, including the child. Gary tried to save her, but the fire spread too fast. I heard he got burned pretty badly trying to get to her room."

"The funeral was heartbreaking," Janet added. "That little girl had been the light of Gary's life. After she died, he just... broke. The man couldn't keep a job, turned to drink, stopped taking care of himself. The insurance company wouldn't pay out. They said the heater was faulty due to negligence."

"State took his land for back taxes about six months ago," Beth continued. "Like I said, a real tragedy."

"Any idea where I can find Gary?"

Both women shook their heads. "No one has seen

or heard from him for almost a year," Janet said. "Some folks think he left town, maybe went to live with relatives somewhere. Others think..." she paused, glancing around. "Others think he might have done something to himself. The grief was eating him alive."

It might be a long shot, but Shea had solved crimes on long shots before. The timing was suspicious. Almost exactly a year since the Richardson fire, right at the beginning of the Christmas season. She returned to Trevor and filled him in on what she'd learned.

"Were you here then?"

"Happened right before I joined the department. Didn't witness it, but did hear about it from the other deputies. Terrible thing. The little girl was trapped in her bedroom when the fire started. Gary was outside gathering firewood for their fireplace." Trevor's expression grew somber. "He blamed himself for not being there, for not having money to replace that old heater."

"Why? You think this Richardson could be our arsonist?"

"I don't know." She sipped her coffee, feeling the warmth spread through her chest. "I do think he warrants us looking into. A man who loses his child in a fire, then watches his life fall apart while the community moves on, well that could create the kind of rage that leads to this."

She gestured toward the smoking ruins. "Find out everything you can about that night. Police reports, fire department records, insurance claims. Try to find him. Ask some questions."

"Okay. I'll do some digging when we return to the office. I'll also check with social services, see if anyone's had contact with him. Maybe check the homeless shelters in the surrounding counties." Trevor pulled out his notebook and made several quick notes. "You coming back with me?"

"In a bit. I wasn't able to get my morning run in, and Heidi needs the exercise." She eyed the track that wrapped around the golf course and disappeared into the woods beyond. The paved trail was one of the development's amenities, designed to give residents a safe place to exercise while enjoying mountain views. "I'll jog here and meet you back at the office."

"Be careful, She. The arsonist might still be in the area..."

"I will be. Come, Heidi."

She tossed the coffee cup into a nearby trash can and set off down the trail. Someone, probably the development's maintenance crew, kept the sidewalk free of snow despite the recent storm. The path was clear and safe, winding past million-dollar homes with their perfectly manicured lawns and expensive landscaping.

Once she entered the woods, the thick canopy of pine and bare-branched hardwoods had kept the snow to just a dusting on the trail. Her gym shoe-covered feet made little noise on the packed earth as she increased her pace.

The woods were peaceful in the early morning, with only the sound of her breathing and Heidi's paws on the trail. Squirrels chattered in the branches overhead, and she caught a glimpse of a red cardinal flashing through the trees. This was why she'd moved to Misty Hollow. She wanted to escape the constant stress of city police work and find some balance in her life.

Heidi stopped suddenly about a quarter-mile into the woods, her ears pricked forward as she stared into the dense undergrowth. The dog's body went rigid, the way it did when she sensed something that didn't belong.

Shea stopped, her breath coming fast in the crisp winter air, forming small clouds that dissipated quickly in the cold. She peered through the shadows between the trees, looking for movement, listening for sounds that didn't fit the forest's natural rhythm. The skin on the back of her neck prickled. They weren't alone in the woods.

"Let's go." She didn't want whoever was watching them to know they'd been discovered. Instead, she'd try to circle around and catch them off guard.

A twig snapped somewhere in the underbrush, the sound sharp and distinct from the natural settling noises of the forest. Heidi growled deep in her throat, a low rumble that meant serious business. Shea put a calming hand on her dog's head, feeling the tension in the animal's muscles.

"Easy, girl," she whispered, then resumed her jog despite the tension settling between her shoulder blades.

The town of Misty Hollow had managed to go almost three months without a murder or theft. The most serious crimes they'd dealt with lately were teenagers drinking beer behind the school and the occasional domestic dispute that ended with someone sleeping on a friend's couch. Now, it seemed they had an arsonist on their hands. Someone who needed to be stopped before more homes were burned and families' holidays ruined.

A rustle in the bushes had her slowing her pace. The sound was too deliberate, too human to be an animal moving through the undergrowth. Did the person watching want her to know they were there? Was this some kind of message or warning?

She reached instinctively for the gun she usually kept on her hip, then realized she'd left her service weapon locked in her truck. She didn't carry when she jogged. The weight threw off her stride, and she'd never felt the need for protection during her morning runs. It might be time to start.

The trail ahead curved to the left, disappearing around a stand of white pines. Beyond that curve, she knew, the path would take her back toward the development and safety. But whoever followed her would know that too. They could easily cut through the woods and intercept her, or simply disappear into the forest's depths before she could get help.

Heidi stayed close to her side now, no longer ranging ahead as she normally did. The dog's instincts were finely tuned after years of working with law enforcement, and her behavior confirmed Shea's growing certainty that they were being deliberately stalked.

As they rounded the curve, Shea made her decision. Instead of continuing toward the development, she would double back through the woods, try to get behind whoever was following them. If it was Gary Richardson, if he was their arsonist, she couldn't let him slip away. Too many lives were at stake, and the Christmas season had only just begun.

Chapter Two

He set the second fire three nights later. The Stevenson's house, famous for its massive light displays and Christmas parties with catered hors d'oeuvres, was the perfect target. From his position crouched behind the towering evergreens that bordered their property, he watched the annual holiday gathering through the floor-to-ceiling windows. Women in cocktail dresses mingled with men in expensive suits, their laughter carrying across the manicured lawn as they sipped champagne and sampled delicate appetizers from silver trays.

The Stevensons had always been the kind of people who had too much—too much money, too much happiness, too much Christmas spirit. Their three-story colonial commanded the best lot in Whispering Pines, with its wraparound porch draped in garland and a ten-foot Noble Fir visible through the front bay window. Outside, their yard resembled a winter wonderland that belonged in a magazine spread. Life-sized reindeer posed beneath twinkling trees, candy cane pathway lights guided visitors to the front door, and an elaborate electric sleigh dominated the center of the lawn.

He remembered when Lilly had pressed her small face against the car window during one of their rare drives through this neighborhood last Christmas. "Daddy, look at all the pretty lights," she had whispered with wonder. He'd promised her that next year, they'd have lights too. Next year, when he saved enough money to replace that cursed space heater.

The gasoline can felt heavier tonight as he approached the display. The timer device he'd constructed in his mountain cabin was crude but effective. A battery pack wired to a heating element, wrapped in cloth soaked with accelerant. He'd learned about delayed ignition from his years working construction, back when controlled burns were sometimes necessary to clear job sites.

When the blaze started twenty minutes later, the electric sleigh burst apart like fireworks, scattering burning fragments across the yard. The carefully wired display became a chain reaction of destruction as one decoration ignited another. Guests screamed as flames raced through the dry pine garland, champagne glasses crashed to the flagstone patio, and the carefully groomed lawn went up in a river of fire that spread toward the house.

He watched from the tree line as people poured from the house in panic, their holiday finery suddenly absurd against the backdrop of chaos. Mrs. Stevenson's silk dress caught on a rose bush as she fled, and her husband stumbled in his patent leather shoes, dropping his phone as he tried to dial 911.

This was better than he'd imagined. Not just destruction, but humiliation. Fear. The same helplessness he'd felt watching everything he loved burn while neighbors stood by doing nothing.

His thoughts drifted to his next target as sirens wailed in the distance. A place in Misty Hollow that would definitely leave a message. Somewhere that served as the heart of the community's daily life. Somewhere they'd never expect. Grinning, he melted into the shadows before the first fire truck arrived, already planning his next strike.

~

Another morning of skipping her pre-dawn jog. Sheriff Shea Callahan had barely slept after the call about the Stevenson fire, spending most of the night reviewing case files and trying to establish a pattern. She exited her truck to the sight of firefighters swarming the massive plantation-style house, their hoses still trained on hot spots that smoldered in the early morning light.

The devastation was more extensive than the Miller house. Where the first fire had been contained to the structure, this one had spread across nearly half an acre. A sleigh in the front yard lay in a melted husk, its metal frame twisted into a sculpture of destruction. The stench of burned plastic and chemicals clung to the air, mixing with the acrid smoke that still rose from the ruins of what had been an award-winning Christmas display.

Fire Chief Bradford approached her, his coat streaked with soot and his eyes rimmed with exhaustion. "Started around ten-thirty, middle of their party. We estimate about forty guests were here when it began. Lucky nobody was seriously hurt, just some minor burns and smoke inhalation."

"Same M.O.?"

"Accelerant, timer device, targeted the Christmas decorations first. But this one was more sophisticated. Multiple ignition points, better coordination. He's learning."

Shea surveyed the scene, noting how the fire had consumed the decorations in a pattern that suggested careful planning. The arsonist had studied this property, mapped out how the blaze would spread for maximum impact.

"The sleigh's wiring must've faulted." Mr. Stevenson appeared at her elbow, his tuxedo jacket wrinkled and stained with ash. Usually impeccably groomed, the bank president looked haggard and confused. "We had the lights installed by professionals last month. Premium components, surge protectors, the whole nine yards. I don't know how this could've happened."

"No." His wife dabbed her eyes with a scarlet

woolen scarf, the expensive fabric now smudged with mascara. Margaret Stevenson was typically composed, the kind of woman who chaired charity committees and hosted political fundraisers. Seeing her disheveled and vulnerable was unsettling. "Someone did this on purpose. Someone who wants to ruin us. We always have the best Christmas displays in town. We've won first place in the holiday lighting contest for five years running. Someone wants to make sure we don't win again."

Shea doubted the motive was that simple, but she nodded sympathetically. "I'm sure it isn't just about the contest, ma'am. We're investigating this as part of a larger pattern."

Spotting Trevor's familiar form near the remains of the sleigh, she excused herself from the distraught couple. Her deputy was crouched low, examining something in the scorched grass .

"Look." Trevor pointed to a discolored patch of lawn about twenty feet from the sleigh's original position. "Accelerant soaked into the grass away from any electrical wiring. This wasn't a short circuit or equipment failure. He doused this whole area, planned for the entire yard to catch fire."

Shea knelt beside him, noting how the burn pattern radiated outward from multiple points. "Professional job. He knows exactly how fire spreads, what materials burn fastest."

She glanced at the stunned partygoers who still

milled about the street despite the cold morning air. Many were filming the aftermath on their phones, no doubt already posting to social media. The story would spread through Misty Hollow faster than the flames had consumed the Stevenson's lawn.

"He waited for the biggest crowd," she continued, pieces clicking into place. "This wasn't just about destroying property. He wants to be seen, wants to create terror. First the Millers, now the Stevensons. Who's next?" Because she'd bet Heidi's favorite squeaky toy on the fact that the fires would continue, most likely with increasing frequency and intensity.

Trevor followed her gaze to the neighboring houses, where Christmas lights that had flickered cheerfully last night now seemed ominous. "Pattern suggests he's targeting the most elaborate displays, the wealthiest families."

"Maybe. Or maybe he's just getting started." Across the street, she noticed lights being switched off as homeowners emerged to survey the damage. Twinkling decorations flickered out one by one as if the arsonist's terror was contagious, spreading fear faster than fire. Shea sighed, understanding their caution but regretting how quickly joy could turn to anxiety.

The crackle of her radio interrupted her thoughts. Fire Chief Bradford's voice cut through the morning air with urgency that made her stomach drop.

"All units, we've got another one. Lucy's Diner on Main Street. Fire truck number two, respond immediately."

Shea exchanged a quick glance with Trevor, both recognizing the escalation. Three fires in less than a week meant they were dealing with someone who was either completely out of control or following a carefully orchestrated plan. Either possibility was terrifying.

"Follow me over?" she asked, already moving toward her truck.

"Right behind you."

They raced for their vehicles, Heidi barking from the passenger seat as sirens wailed and the fire truck accelerated down the street.

By the time they arrived at Lucy's, the flames had been extinguished by Frank Morrison, a truck driver who'd been making an early morning delivery to the hardware store next door. All that remained was a scorched Christmas tree visible through the diner's large front window, along with a spider's web of cracks in the glass where heat had stressed the pane beyond its breaking point.

The damage was relatively minor compared to the previous fires, but the location sent a clear message. Lucy's Diner wasn't just another business. It was the unofficial town hall where residents gathered for coffee and gossip, where city council meetings were planned over pie, where newcomers were welcomed and longtime residents held court. Attacking Lucy's was like striking at the heart of Misty Hollow itself.

After searching the area around the building, Fire

Chief Bradford emerged from behind the diner carrying evidence that confirmed their worst fears. He showed them a melted timer device, its plastic housing warped but still recognizable. "Battery pack, electrical wires, accelerant reservoir, classic delayed ignition system. Whoever built this knows electronics and has experience with demolition work."

Shea exhaled slowly, her breath forming small clouds in the chilly air as she processed the implications. "He's testing us now. First the house fires to establish his capabilities, now this to see how fast we can respond. He's studying our reaction times."

Trevor nodded grimly. "Lucy's Diner is a town icon. Everyone knows this place, everyone comes here. This is a message, but what's he trying to say?"

Before Shea could respond, Lucy burst through the diner's rear entrance, flour dusting the front of her red apron and fury blazing in her dark eyes. At sixty-two, Lucy had weathered every crisis Misty Hollow had faced in the past. She was the kind of woman who fed people during funerals and stayed open during blizzards to serve coffee to snowplow drivers.

"I was in the back kitchen working on today's bread." Her voice shook with anger rather than fear. "If I'd been out front cleaning tables like usual, I could've died. And if this psychopath thinks he's going to scare me into closing my doors, well, he'd better think again. I've been serving this community since before half these houses were built. I'm not running away."

"I understand your feelings, Lucy, and I admire your courage." Shea placed a reassuring hand on the woman's shoulder, feeling the tension in her muscles. "But I need you to be smart about this. Keep the Christmas decorations to a minimum for now, okay? They seem to be triggering these attacks."

Lucy's expression softened as she looked at the charred remains of her holiday display. The tree had been decorated with handmade ornaments contributed by local school children over the years, each one representing a memory and a connection to the community.

"Footprints over here," Trevor called from where he and Heidi stood near a bare maple tree behind the building. The dog had been trained to detect accelerants, and her behavior suggested she'd found something significant. Trevor was already photographing the evidence with his phone, documenting everything before the scene could be contaminated.

Shea joined them, studying the impressions in the soft earth. The prints were clear despite the overnight frost, pressed deep into the mud near the diner's back door. "Man's size twelve, heavy work boots with a distinctive tread pattern. Could be our arsonist."

The boots looked expensive—the kind worn by construction workers or outdoorsmen who needed reliable footwear in all weather conditions. The tread was worn but not completely smooth, suggesting someone who worked physically demanding jobs but took care of his equipment.

Trevor measured the prints with a ruler from his kit, noting the depth and spacing. "Stride suggests someone around six feet tall, probably weighing between one-sixty and one-eighty pounds. He was moving slowly, deliberately. No signs of running or panic."

Shea rubbed her hands down her face, feeling the weight of responsibility settling on her shoulders like a lead blanket. The Stevenson's fire had shown the arsonist escalating from private destruction to public spectacle, demonstrating his willingness to endanger innocent people for dramatic effect. Lucy's Diner proved his tactical awareness and growing confidence. The combination suggested someone intelligent, methodical, and completely committed to his campaign of terror.

"Could this be some kid acting out?" Trevor asked, though his tone suggested he already knew the answer.

"I don't think so. The sophistication of the devices, the careful planning, the symbolic targeting—this is someone older. Someone with technical knowledge and a deep, personal grudge against this town." She studied the footprint casts Trevor was making, already planning to send them to the state forensics lab for analysis.

The pattern became clearer with each fire. The arsonist wasn't choosing targets randomly. He selected symbols of Christmas joy and community prosperity, places and people who represented everything he'd lost or never had. The question was whether they could identify him before his campaign of revenge claimed its first life.

As if reading her thoughts, Trevor straightened from his work and fixed her with a worried expression. "Shea, what if stopping property damage isn't his end game? What if he's building up to something worse?"

Shea didn't answer immediately, but the same fear had been gnawing at her since the first fire. She'd learned that criminals who escalated this quickly rarely stopped until they were caught. Given the arsonist's apparent technical skills and intimate knowledge of the community, she suspected they were racing against a very short clock.

Chapter Three

Rumors spread faster than the flames that had consumed three properties in less than a week. Shea stared at the stack of messages covering her desk—each one a different theory, accusation, or complaint from increasingly panicked residents. The pink message slips had multiplied overnight, her dispatcher fielding calls from dawn until well past midnight.

One woman swore she saw a man in black running away from the Stevenson home, though she'd been three blocks away and wearing reading glasses that hadn't been updated in five years. Another insisted it was a gang initiation, citing a crime show she'd watched where similar fires marked territory in urban areas. The message that cut Shea deepest was: "Caller says Trevor should be in charge because he has more experience in the town of Misty Hollow and understands local dynamics better than an outsider."

How quickly they forgot the killers she'd brought

to justice, the dangers she'd eliminated from their community. It seemed she was only as good as her most recent case, only as competent as her latest success. The weight of constant scrutiny pressed down on her shoulders, heavier with each passing hour that the arsonist remained free.

Still, every lead would have to be investigated, no matter how ridiculous or personally insulting. In small-town law enforcement, ignoring even the most far-fetched tip could mean missing the crucial detail that broke a case wide open. She donned her winter coat, checked that her service weapon was secure in its holster, and called for Heidi to follow.

"Are we heading out?" Trevor glanced up from his desk where he'd been reviewing fire department reports and insurance claims. Dark circles under his eyes revealed he'd been working as late as she had, cross-referencing victim lists and examining burn patterns.

"Yes. I've received some leads that I seriously doubt will amount to anything productive, but we have to check them out anyway." She tossed him the keys to squad car number two, their newer vehicle with better heating and more reliable radio equipment. "You drive. I need to review these witness statements while we're mobile."

He caught the keys mid-air. "Where to first?"

"Main Street Bakery. Mrs. Winfield claims she witnessed our suspect fleeing the scene."

The drive took less than five minutes, but Shea

used the time to organize the various tips and sightings into categories—possible, improbable, and completely ridiculous. Unfortunately, most fell into the latter two classifications.

Mrs. Winfield was waiting for them when they arrived, practically vibrating with excitement behind the bakery's glass counter. At seventy-three, Eleanor Winfield had appointed herself the unofficial neighborhood watch coordinator for downtown Misty Hollow. She leaned over the counter before they could even introduce themselves, flour dusting her apron and determination gleaming in her watery blue eyes.

"I saw him clear as day," she began without preamble. "Dressed all in black from head to toe, broad shoulders like a linebacker. A tall man, maybe six-two or six-three. He was definitely not from around here—had that city way of moving, you know? Purposeful but sneaky."

Shea shot Trevor an exasperated look before turning back to the older woman. "Mrs. Winfield, you saw all these details in the middle of the night? The Stevenson fire occurred around ten-thirty PM, and there's no streetlight between here and their property."

"I've got excellent night vision, Sheriff. Always have. My late husband used to say I could spot a barn owl at midnight." Mrs. Winfield's chin jutted forward defensively. "I was taking out the evening's trash when I saw this figure moving through the Stevenson's yard like he owned the place."

"How can you be absolutely certain the man you allegedly observed isn't from Misty Hollow?" Shea kept her tone professional despite her growing frustration. "You live three blocks away."

The woman frowned, as if the question itself was insulting. "Sheriff, I know everyone in this town and the surrounding county. I've lived here my entire seventy-three years, born in the house where my grandmother delivered me. Even the newcomers from that fancy development come in here for my apple turnovers and Christmas cookies. I pride myself on recognizing faces."

She gestured toward Trevor with a flour-dusted finger. "Why aren't you writing this down, Deputy? This is important information."

"Right, absolutely." Trevor's lips twitched slightly as he pulled a small notepad from his shirt pocket and began scribbling, though Shea suspected he was doodling rather than recording Mrs. Winfield's dubious testimony.

Their next stop was Misty Hollow High School, a red-brick building constructed in the 1960s that housed grades seven through twelve. The school counselor, Patricia Hayes, met them in her cramped office, decorated with motivational posters and a small artificial Christmas tree that looked almost defiant, given the current climate of fear.

She nodded gravely as Shea mentioned the message about gang initiation. "I want to emphasize that I'm only reporting what I've overheard in conversations between students and faculty. We don't actually have any gang activity at this school, but several teenagers are speculating that one has come here from Little Rock to establish territory."

"All the way to Misty Hollow?" Shea frowned, calculating the distance. "That would require significant resources and planning. It seems far-fetched considering the time and effort it would take to travel here for what amounts to vandalism."

"Like I said, Sheriff, I'm simply repeating what's being discussed in the hallways and faculty lounge. I don't personally subscribe to these theories." The counselor adjusted her reading glasses and folded her hands carefully on her desk. "What's more concerning to me is the psychological impact on our younger students. I've heard from colleagues at the elementary school that children are asking their parents if it's safe enough for Santa Claus to come to their houses this year. Some are refusing to hang stockings or put up Christmas trees."

The thought of children living in fear during what should be the most magical time of year made Shea's stomach tighten. This was exactly what the arsonist wanted. Not just property damage, but the destruction of joy and tradition that bound communities together.

"Thank you for your concern and for reporting what you've heard," Shea said, standing to leave. "We'll certainly look into all possibilities." She was beginning to sound like a broken record, giving the same diplomatic response to increasingly ridiculous theories.

"Barbershop next?" Trevor opened the driver's side door and leaned in to pat Heidi, who waited patiently in the back seat. The German Shepherd's ears perked up at his attention, though she remained alert and focused as always.

"Yes, even though it's probably another complete waste of our time and taxpayer money." Shea slid into the passenger seat and clicked her seatbelt into place, already dreading the conversation awaiting them.

The barbershop occupied a narrow storefront that hadn't changed much since the 1950s, complete with red and white striped pole and vintage barber chairs. Conversation ceased abruptly when they stepped inside, creating an uncomfortable silence that felt almost hostile. Five heads turned to stare coldly at Shea, their expressions ranging from skeptical to openly dismissive.

"She's green as grass," someone muttered from the back of the shop, "but I guess she's all we've got right now." An older man wearing a traditional white barber's apron stepped from behind a curtain that separated the work area from a small storage room. His eyes widened in apparent surprise at the sight of Shea, as if he hadn't expected her to actually show up. "Oh. Sheriff."

"I heard that you gentlemen are concerned about my ability to handle these arson cases." Shea tilted her head slightly, keeping her expression impassive despite the anger building in her chest. "I want to guarantee you that I am fully capable of solving this crime and bringing the perpetrator to justice. Now, unless you have actual facts to report rather than speculation and gossip, please refrain from calling the sheriff's office every few hours. You're tying up emergency lines when citizens with genuine information are trying to get through."

"Well, here's something that might actually matter," the man from the back said, ignoring Shea entirely and directing his comments to Trevor. "Hey there, Deputy Bolton."

"Mr. Blackwell." Trevor gave a respectful nod to the man who'd been cutting hair in Misty Hollow for nearly forty years. "What information do you have for us?"

Fine. If Blackwell wanted to speak only to Trevor, she'd stand quietly and let him run with it. It wasn't the first time men had overlooked her authority because she was a woman, and it probably wouldn't be the last. The key was getting information, regardless of wounded pride.

"The board of directors at the Methodist Church held an emergency meeting last night," Blackwell began, setting a stack of freshly laundered white towels on the counter next to his chair. "They're seriously considering canceling the children's Christmas pageant that's been a tradition for over fifty years. Too worried about having that many families gathered in one place with all those candles and decorations."

He crossed his arms over his chest, his expression grim. "The Baptist Church is having similar discussions about shutting down its annual candlelight vigil on Christmas Eve. Reverend Williams said they'd be sitting ducks with all those open flames and people packed together in the sanctuary. The Catholic Parish is the only congregation refusing to cancel any holiday festivities. Father O'Malley said they will not let fear steal their light or compromise their faith."

Blackwell's voice grew more intense. "Sheriff, you need to stop all of this madness before Christmas gets completely canceled in Misty Hollow."

"We're doing everything possible," Trevor responded diplomatically. "The sheriff has been working eighteen-hour days, going over every piece of evidence and following up on every lead, no matter how small."

"What exactly do you know so far?" Another man chimed in from his position near the front window. "Folks are getting desperate for some kind of progress report."

"We cannot discuss specifics of an ongoing investigation," Trevor replied, sticking to protocol. "But I can assure you we're making progress and following several promising leads."

Shea had heard enough. The speculation and criticism were only adding to the community's panic while providing no useful information. "I'll be holding a press conference outside the sheriff's office this afternoon at five o'clock," she announced, then turned and walked out before anyone could respond.

"Hold up, Shea." Trevor caught up with her on the sidewalk, pulling out his smartphone. "Before we head back, one of the men inside showed me something you need to see."

He handed her the phone, displaying a news article from the regional paper that served three counties. The headline made her stomach drop: "Holiday Terror: Sheriff Callahan Trails Arsonist's Blaze." Below the sensationalized text was a photo of a young reporter she didn't recognize, his eager face practically glowing with ambition as he stared at the camera.

The article's opening paragraph was even worse: "Another fire, another missed opportunity to apprehend Misty Hollow's Christmas arsonist. Is Sheriff Callahan in over her head? Long-time residents say she's consistently one step behind the perpetrator, arriving at crime scenes only after maximum damage has been done."

Shea felt her jaw clench as she read further. The reporter had interviewed several unnamed sources who questioned her investigative methods, her commitment to the community, and her overall competence. None of them had bothered to mention the crimes she'd successfully solved or the improvements she'd made to the department's efficiency and community relations.

"How quickly they forget," she muttered, handing the phone back to Trevor. She bore the physical and mental scars of bringing down killers.

"Could've been worse," Trevor said, attempting to lighten the mood. "They could be calling you the Grinch and me your faithful elf helper."

"Why would they call me the Grinch?" Shea frowned at him over the hood of the patrol car. "Because I haven't put up any Christmas decorations at my house?"

"Hey, don't feel bad about that. I never manage anything more elaborate than a three-foot artificial tree, and half the time it doesn't even get decorated because I'm too busy with work." He flashed a grin that was meant to be encouraging. "Last year, I think I hung exactly four ornaments before giving up."

Shea gave a bitter laugh that held no humor. "At this point, I'd consider even that a major accomplishment."

At exactly five o'clock, Shea stood outside the sheriff's office facing a small crowd of reporters and residents. A cold wind whipped down Main Street, making her eyes water and cutting through her winter coat like it was made of tissue paper. Several journalists shivered under thick parkas, their camera operators stamping their feet to maintain circulation. Camera flashes popped intermittently, creating harsh white bursts that left temporary spots in her vision.

Trevor and Fire Chief Bradford flanked her,

presenting a united front of law enforcement and emergency services. The fire chief had insisted on participating, arguing that community confidence needed to be restored through visible cooperation between agencies.

Shea took a deep breath, feeling the cold air burn her lungs. "Citizens of Misty Hollow, I want to assure you that we will stop this arsonist. Our community must not surrender to fear or allow terrorism to dictate how we live our lives. Whoever is setting these fires—if you're listening—understand this: your flames will not consume this town. We will find you, and we will bring you to justice."

"Those are just empty words, Sheriff!" someone shouted from the back of the crowd. "What are you actually doing besides showing up after the damage is done?"

Shea squared her shoulders and maintained eye contact with the cameras, refusing to be baited into a defensive response. After delivering a few more prepared statements about ongoing investigations and community safety measures, she turned and walked back into the sheriff's office with as much dignity as she could muster.

"You looked strong and confident up there," Trevor said once they were inside. "Very professional under pressure."

"Honestly? I feel like I'm hanging on by my fingernails." Shea slumped into a desk chair, suddenly exhausted by the weight of everyone's expectations and the constant pressure to solve an increasingly complex case.

Deputy Butler chose that moment to approach their desks, carrying a thin manila folder that represented hours of investigative work. "Here's what we've managed to find out about Gary Richardson so far. After his house burned down and his daughter died in the fire, the man essentially became a drifter. There are scattered reports from various law enforcement agencies that he vowed to get revenge on this town because of what he perceived as a complete lack of help and support after the tragedy."

"That's it?" Shea looked up from the sparse file contents. "That's practically nothing. We need to locate this man so we can question him properly, examine his current mental state, and determine if he has the means and opportunity to commit these crimes."

"We're still actively searching, Sheriff. Every law enforcement agency in a three-state area has his description and last known information. We'll find him eventually." Butler returned to his desk, leaving Shea feeling more frustrated than ever.

"When this whole nightmare is over," Trevor said, settling into his chair and logging into his computer, "I'm personally buying you a Christmas tree. Nothing fancy—no lights, no tinsel, no ornaments that could catch fire. Just a plain, safe pine tree that smells like the holidays should."

Shea found herself smirking despite her exhaustion. "You'd better remember that promise when the time comes."

"I always keep my promises," he replied, his hand accidentally brushing against hers as he reached for a pen. "Always."

Silence lingered in the office, the air between them suddenly heavy with unspoken words and possibilities that neither was quite ready to acknowledge. The moment stretched until it became almost uncomfortable, charged with the kind of tension that develops between partners who've worked closely together through crisis after crisis.

Before either could break the spell, Shea's radio crackled to life with the harsh static that preceded emergency calls. The dispatcher's voice cut through the quiet office like a knife.

"All units, we have fire."

Chapter Four

A biting frost blanketed Misty Hollow like a shroud, coating every surface with crystalline ice that crunched underfoot and turned the world into a frozen wasteland. Sheriff Shea Callahan shoved her hands under her armpits to keep them warm, waiting impatiently for her truck's heater to finally kick in. The dashboard vents breathed out nothing but cold air that made her shiver harder, despite her heavy winter coat and wool-lined gloves.

Finally, giving up on waiting for mechanical mercy, she put the truck in drive and headed toward Misty Pines Park. The roads were treacherous with black ice, forcing her to drive slower than usual while emergency lights from fire trucks and patrol cars painted the early evening darkness in alternating waves of red and blue.

Despite another radio call confirming that this latest fire had been contained to a single trash can, they finally had something different—a suspect in custody and actual witnesses. She hoped they'd get their first real clue this time, but doubted whoever had set this small fire was their true arsonist. No, that person wouldn't waste time on such insignificant destruction. He, or she, wanted much more than a burnt garbage receptacle and scattered debris.

The real arsonist craved terror, chaos, and the complete destruction of everything that brought joy to Misty Hollow during the Christmas season. A trash can fire was beneath their twisted ambitions.

Trevor waited for her near the park entrance, his breath forming small clouds as he spoke into his radio. The patrol cars' headlights illuminated the scene like stage lighting, casting long shadows across the playground equipment and frozen grass.

"The two witnesses are huddled under the gazebo trying to stay warm," he reported as she approached. "The young man who actually set the fire is being detained near the playground slide. Fire department says the flames were easily contained—mostly paper and cardboard, nothing that spread beyond the metal receptacle."

"What else do we know?" She fell into step beside him as they walked toward the Victorian-style gazebo that served as the park's centerpiece. Her boots crunched through frost-covered leaves, each step echoing in the unnaturally quiet evening.

"I've been waiting for you before questioning

anyone officially," Trevor replied, pulling the collar of his coat higher against the wind that whipped across the open space. "Man, it's absolutely frigid out here. Temperature must've dropped twenty degrees since this afternoon."

"Colder than it should be for this time of evening," she agreed, glancing toward the blackened trash can. Christmas candy wrappers in bright reds and greens, along with metallic tinsel scraps, littered the ground in a radius around the container. The debris looked oddly festive despite the circumstances, like confetti after a party.

When they reached the gazebo, Shea could see two teenage boys sitting close together on the built-in benches, sharing body heat and looking thoroughly miserable. She recognized them both from a previous investigation—the drowning of several high school girls at the lake last summer, a tragic accident that had required interviewing most of the junior and senior classes.

"Good evening, gentlemen. I'm Sheriff Callahan, and this is Deputy Bolton," she said, introducing herself and Trevor with professional courtesy. "I need you to state your full names for the record, please."

"I'm Justin Baker," the blond boy said, his voice carrying the nervous energy of someone who'd never been involved in a police investigation. "This is Marc Snyder." He jerked his head toward his dark-haired companion, who nodded acknowledgment while keeping his hands buried deep in his jacket pockets.

"We were walking home from youth group at the Methodist Church when we spotted the flames," Justin continued, his words coming out in quick bursts between chattering teeth. "We immediately called 911 like we were supposed to. We panicked a little bit, I guess, but we tried to do the right thing."

"No, you absolutely did the right thing," Shea assured them, noting how young and frightened they looked. "Calling emergency services was exactly what you should have done in that situation. Do you know the boy who set the fire?"

"Yes, ma'am," Marc spoke up for the first time, his voice barely above a whisper. "That's Jake Thompson over there. We all play varsity football together during the season. He's our starting quarterback." He paused, looking uncertain. "We never thought he could be the one doing all this arson stuff around town. Jake's not like that."

"I seriously doubt he is either," Shea said, giving both boys a stern but reassuring look. "But I need you to understand something important. Don't start spreading rumors or speculation about this incident. The public will know who the real arsonist is once we apprehend him, and it won't be through gossip or assumptions. You two go give your complete statements to Officer Henderson over there by the patrol car."

She motioned for Trevor to follow her across the

playground to where a third teenager sat on the bottom of the slide, looking thoroughly dejected and scared. Jake Thompson was smaller than she'd expected for a quarterback, maybe sixteen years old with sandy brown hair and the kind of baby face that made him look even younger.

"I was only trying to start a warming fire so my friends and I could hang out without freezing to death," Jake said before they could even speak, the words tumbling out in a rush of nervous energy. "That's all this was about, I swear on my mother's grave."

"Where exactly are these friends of yours?" Shea glanced around the empty park, seeing nothing but emergency personnel and playground equipment. "I don't see anyone else here."

"They haven't shown up yet, and I don't think they will now," Jake replied miserably, hunching over and pulling his oversized hoodie closer around his thin frame. "They probably saw all the police cars and fire trucks and decided to bail. Can't really blame them for that."

"Why were you planning to meet here in the first place?" She gestured for an officer to bring the boy a blanket, noting how he was shivering almost uncontrollably in the cold.

"I... I snuck some beers from my dad's garage refrigerator earlier today," Jake admitted, his face flushing red with embarrassment. "That's all we were gonna do, I promise. Just drink a couple of beers and try to stay warm. Nothing illegal or dangerous."

"Underage drinking is illegal." Trevor retrieved a forest-green backpack from a nearby picnic table and unzipped it with deliberate slowness, revealing its contents for everyone to see. "Care to explain the lighter fluid, wooden matches, and this flyer for the upcoming Christmas festival downtown?"

Jake's eyes widened as he saw his possessions displayed like evidence at a crime scene. "I already told you I was trying to start a fire to keep warm while we waited. I pulled some of those festival flyers off telephone poles around town to use as kindling in case there wasn't enough paper trash in the can to get flames going properly." His voice cracked slightly with stress. "I'm not the psycho who's been setting fire to people's houses, Sheriff. I would never do anything like that to hurt innocent families."

Shea studied the boy's face carefully, looking for signs of deception but finding only genuine fear and confusion. She didn't think Jake Thompson was their arsonist either, but it wouldn't hurt him to spend a few hours in the interrogation room at the station before his parents arrived to collect him. Sometimes a scare was exactly what teenagers needed to straighten out their priorities.

"We're taking you into custody, Jake," she said firmly. "What you've done here tonight is serious, regardless of your intentions. Unauthorized fires in public spaces are dangerous and illegal."

Deputy Butler approached, carrying a thick wool blanket, his expression grim as he surveyed the scene. "Parents with young children cleared out of the park as soon as this boy's fire started burning," he reported. "I tried to ask some basic questions about what they might have seen, but no one wanted to stick around long enough to talk. They're genuinely terrified, Sheriff. The whole community is walking on eggshells."

"I don't blame them for being scared." Shea watched as Trevor placed Jake in handcuffs, wrapped the blanket around the teenager's shoulders, and then escorted him toward the nearest squad car. "But this kid isn't the person we're searching for."

"I don't think so either," Butler agreed, "but the general public is going to want a scapegoat. Someone to blame for all this chaos and fear. They need to feel like progress is being made."

"It won't be Jake Thompson," Shea said with finality. "Not if I can help it." The boy might have made a stupid decision tonight, but he didn't deserve to become the target of an entire town's frustration and panic.

The next morning dawned gray and bitter, with heavy clouds promising more snow before evening. Shea cruised slowly down Main Street in her patrol truck, eyes constantly scanning for anything unusual or out of place. She couldn't remember a time in her time as sheriff when the downtown area had felt so deserted and unwelcoming.

The usual morning bustle was utterly absent. No mothers pushing strollers toward the library, no elderly men gathering outside the hardware store to discuss weather and politics, no high school students walking to their part-time jobs at local businesses. The sidewalks were empty except for occasional footprints in the frost, and many storefronts that should have been bustling with Christmas shoppers remained dark behind locked doors.

She pulled into the small parking lot beside Lucy's Diner and frowned at the sight of fresh plywood nailed over the large front window. A stark reminder of the recent arson attempt. The wood looked raw and yellow against the diner's cheerful red brick exterior, like a bandage over a wound that hadn't properly healed.

Inside, the atmosphere was subdued and tense. Only a handful of customers occupied the tables and booths that were usually packed by this time of morning. Shea chose a booth near the back wall with a clear view of both the front entrance and the kitchen door, told Heidi to lie down quietly under the table, and glanced at the hand-written whiteboard advertising the morning special—a tall stack of buttermilk pancakes with maple syrup and bacon.

"Morning, Sheriff," Lucy called from behind the counter, her smile looking forced and tired. Dark circles under her eyes suggested she hadn't been sleeping well since the attack on her diner. "Is Deputy Bolton joining you for breakfast today?"

"Yes, he should be walking through that door any minute now," Shea replied, studying Lucy's face with concern. "Are you holding up okay? You look exhausted."

Lucy's professional mask slipped slightly as she heaved a deep sigh and slid uninvited into the booth across from Shea. "Honestly? I'm barely keeping it together. Half the businesses on Main Street are saying they're going to start closing at five o'clock each day instead of staying open for evening customers. The fire department announced yesterday that they're canceling their annual Santa visit with the antique fire truck—you know, that event where kids get to sit on Santa's lap and tour the equipment? Been a tradition for thirty years."

She rubbed her temples as if fighting a headache. "Two of the local churches have already canceled their children's choir rehearsals because parents are too scared to let kids gather in groups after dark. This maniac is killing Christmas in Misty Hollow, Sheriff. People are demanding that this nightmare be stopped before it's too late to save the holiday season."

"There's a town hall meeting scheduled for tonight at seven," Shea said. "I'll be there to address everyone's concerns and provide updates on our investigation." Again, she thought grimly. How many times would she have to stand in front of frightened residents and promise them something she wasn't sure she could deliver?

Relief flooded through her as she spotted Trevor

entering the diner, stomping his boots on the mat, and unwinding a thick scarf from around his neck. His cheeks were red from the cold, but he managed a genuine smile as he spotted their table.

"I'll definitely be there tonight," Lucy said, standing to greet her other regular customer. "Y'all know what you want to eat this morning?"

"Biscuits and chocolate gravy," Shea decided, opting for comfort food that might help settle her increasingly nervous stomach. "And could you scramble two eggs with no seasoning for Heidi, please?"

"The buttermilk pancake special sounds perfect." Trevor slid into the booth and pulled off his heavy winter coat. Once Lucy had left to place their orders with the kitchen, he leaned forward and lowered his voice. "So, are you ready for tonight's town meeting? Should be interesting."

"As ready as anyone can be to face an angry mob," Shea replied with dark humor. "The problem is we still don't know anything concrete. We have theories, suspicions, and a growing pile of circumstantial evidence, but nothing that would stand up in court."

"You really don't think Jake Thompson is our culprit?" Trevor asked, though his tone suggested he already knew the answer.

"Of course not. The person we're hunting is much smarter, more calculating and methodical than a sixteen-year-old kid who panics when he sees police cars." She crossed her arms on the table and leaned forward. "Are you fully aware of how badly this town is shutting down? Lucy just told me about all the canceled events and early closures."

Trevor nodded grimly. "I've been hearing similar reports all week. The elementary school is considering canceling their holiday concert, the library stopped their evening story times, and I heard the senior center might close entirely until after New Year's."

"We've got exactly three weeks until Christmas." The weight of that deadline pressed down on her shoulders. "We can catch him before then. We have to."

She wished she possessed even half of Trevor's apparent optimism. After a breakfast that neither of them truly enjoyed, they headed back to the sheriff's office to handle routine administrative duties and continue their increasingly frustrating online search for any trace of Gary Richardson.

By the time evening arrived and the town hall meeting was scheduled to begin, frustration and desperation boiled through Shea like acid in her veins. Richardson remained a ghost—no recent arrests, no employment records, no social services contacts, no paper trail of any kind. It was as if he'd vanished from the face of the earth after his daughter's death.

Head held high and shoulders squared with determination, she marched between the rows of folding chairs that filled the community center to capacity. The podium had been set up at the front of the room like a judge's bench, and she'd no sooner taken her position behind it than the shouting began from every direction.

"Just arrest the Thompson boy already!" someone called from the middle of the crowd.

"He's obviously a menace to this community!" another voice added.

A woman near the front stood up, her face flushed with emotion. "My children can't sleep through the night anymore. They're absolutely terrified that the Christmas tree in our living room will suddenly catch fire and burn the house down with all of us inside."

"You promised us safety and security, Sheriff," an elderly man accused from his seat near the back. "But all we've gotten is more fear and more fires. When is this going to end?"

Shea gripped the podium with both hands, feeling the smooth wood beneath her palms as she tried to project calm authority despite the chaos surrounding her. "I hear and understand your fear. I feel it too— every single day. But I will not rush to judgment or condemn an innocent person just to appease public opinion. Jake Thompson is not the person we're looking for. The true arsonist is still out there, and my department will stop him."

The mayor stood slowly from his seat in the front row, his political smile replaced by the stern expression he wore when conducting official business. "The people of this community want results, Sheriff. They deserve action, not more empty promises. The vast majority of residents believe that boy is guilty, and we want him formally charged with these crimes."

Shea met the mayor's challenging gaze with a steady one of her own, refusing to be intimidated by political pressure. "I won't convict an innocent teenager in the court of public opinion, Mayor. When I bring you the real arsonist, you'll have absolutely no doubt it's the right person."

After the contentious meeting finally ended, the mayor cornered Shea near the exit, speaking in low tones that wouldn't carry to the lingering crowd members.

"Listen to me carefully, Sheriff. Arrest the Thompson boy publicly. Make a big show of it for the cameras and reporters. Give these terrified people some sense of peace and progress, even if it's temporary." The mayor's voice carried the hard edge of political calculation. "If you're absolutely certain he isn't the guilty party, you can always release him quietly after a day or two. At minimum, the boy will have learned a valuable lesson about playing with fire."

Shea felt her stomach twist with distaste, but she recognized the political reality of her situation. "Fine. Maybe by doing so, it will calm the panic enough to buy my department some time to find the real culprit."

The next evening's local news broadcast showed Jake Thompson being led from his family's modest home in handcuffs, his young face twisted with anguish and confusion as cameras captured every moment of his humiliation.

"I didn't do it!" he shouted toward the reporters and neighbors who had gathered on the sidewalk. "Sheriff Callahan, you know I didn't do this! Please don't let them blame me for something I didn't do."

His mother collapsed sobbing on the front porch, begging Shea through her tears to believe in her son's innocence, to protect him from a community that had already decided his guilt. The woman's anguish was visible and heartbreaking, a poignant reminder of how quickly justice could become vengeance in small towns where fear often overrode reason.

Without saying a word in response to the family's pleas, Shea turned away from the scene and returned to her patrol truck, feeling like she'd betrayed everything she believed about law enforcement and protecting the innocent.

~

Miles away in his mountain cabin, he watched Jake Thompson's mugshot flash across the evening news broadcast, his lips curling into a smile of genuine amusement. The boy looked terrified and confused, exactly like a scapegoat should look when faced with crimes he couldn't comprehend.

"They actually think it's over," he murmured to the empty room, shaking his head at their collective stupidity. "They honestly believe a nervous kid with sweaty palms and a pocketful of matches could have planned and executed something this sophisticated? Let them cling to that delusion. They'll discover the truth soon enough."

He rose from his makeshift chair and moved to the cracked window, staring down at the twinkling lights of Misty Hollow spread out in the valley below. "When I burn the very heart of their precious community, when I take away the thing they value most, they'll finally understand it was me. They'll know that Gary Richardson isn't finished with them yet."

Later that night, he left the cabin and drove his rusted pickup truck into town, parking several blocks away from his intended destination. He walked the empty streets completely unnoticed, hood pulled low over his face, heavy work boots crunching on the frozen ground with each deliberate step.

He passed house after house with unplugged Christmas lights, porches stripped bare of wreaths and decorations, windows dark and curtained against the night. The sight filled him with satisfaction so deep it was almost physical pleasure. No smiles on the faces of the few people he encountered. No songs of joy drifting from warm homes. No children playing in yards decorated with holiday cheer.

The residents of Misty Hollow now walked in the same fear he had lived with since Lilly's death. The terror of losing everything precious without warning. That knowledge pleased him more than anything had in over a year.

"This is just the beginning," he whispered into the cold night air, his breath forming small clouds that dissipated quickly in the darkness. "They still don't understand the hole she left in the world. They haven't suffered nearly enough for their indifference."

But they would. Very soon, they would understand exactly what it felt like to lose the thing they loved most at the time when joy should have been at its peak. Christmas morning would bring them a gift they'd never forget. The same devastation that had consumed his life when no one in this town had cared enough to help.

Chapter Five

Shea joined Trevor on Main Street, positioning themselves strategically near the hardware store where they could monitor the entire square. The two law enforcement officers stood off to the side on high alert as town residents gradually gathered for what had been Misty Hollow's most cherished annual tradition for over forty years. Every available deputy in the department had been deployed throughout the crowd, their eyes constantly scanning faces and searching for anything suspicious or out of place.

Shea didn't think moving ahead with the annual Christmas tree lighting was a wise decision under the current circumstances, but Mayor Ferguson had insisted that canceling would send the message that the arsonist had won. "We can't let fear dictate our lives," he'd argued during their heated discussion that morning. "This community needs something positive to rally around."

Against her better judgment, she'd agreed to provide security rather than fight a political battle she couldn't win. Now, watching the vulnerable families gathering in the open square, she wondered if she'd made a terrible mistake.

Frost dusted the asphalt street like powdered sugar, each crystal twinkling beneath strings of multicolored bulbs that had been draped carefully from lamppost to lamppost earlier that afternoon. Local vendors had set up small carts selling steaming cups of hot cocoa topped with marshmallows and bags of roasted chestnuts that filled the air with rich, nutty aromas. Children bundled in bright knit hats and thick mittens chased each other between the adults. At the same time, parents huddled together in wool scarves, stamping their boots against the bitter cold and casting nervous, furtive glances around the perimeter of the gathering.

"Smaller crowd than usual?" Shea asked, noting the gaps between family groups that would normally be packed shoulder to shoulder.

"About half the size of last year's turnout," Trevor confirmed, his breath forming small clouds as he spoke. "A lot of people are staying home, but enough showed up to make me nervous. Too many potential targets in one location."

The centerpiece of the celebration was a magnificent forty-foot spruce that towered over the town square, its branches wrapped in thousands of twinkling white lights that had taken the volunteer fire department most of the previous day to install. A golden star gleamed proudly at the very top, visible from blocks away and serving as the crown jewel of the display.

Mayor Ferguson approached the microphone that had been set up on a small platform decorated with red and green bunting. His voice boomed across the square with forced cheerfulness that didn't quite mask the underlying tension everyone felt. "Citizens of Misty Hollow, our town has always stood together through good times and bad. No fire, no fear, no criminal will take away our Christmas spirit or destroy the traditions that bind us as a community. Tonight, we light this tree as a beacon of hope that will shine through the darkness."

Scattered but polite applause rippled through the crowd, parents hugging their children a little tighter as the mayor raised his hand dramatically toward the towering spruce. The moment felt pregnant with anticipation and barely contained anxiety.

Shea held her breath as she gripped Trevor's arm unconsciously. He placed his warm hand over hers reassuringly, but kept his intense gaze fixed on the tree and the crowd surrounding it.

A tiny spark suddenly flashed at the star, barely visible but definitely there. The entire crowd seemed to hold its collective breath, sensing that something was wrong but not yet understanding what they were witnessing.

Then, without warning, the entire top section of the tree erupted in a massive fireball that sent flames surging downward like liquid fire. The inferno swallowed ornaments, garland, and lights with terrifying speed, consuming forty years of community tradition in a matter of seconds. A thunderous boom rattled storefront windows as the heat-stressed branches cracked and splintered, hurling burning embers across the square like deadly confetti. Glass ornaments exploded like grenades, sending sharp fragments flying in all directions.

Mothers shrieked in terror, their screams piercing the night air as they grabbed for their children. A baby stroller tipped over in the sudden crush of panicking people, spilling a crying toddler onto the cold pavement. Adults trampled past in their desperation to escape the falling debris.

Trevor immediately released Shea's hand and dove through the chaos, scooping the wailing child into his strong arms and hunching over her protectively to shield her from the rain of sparks and burning fragments. His quick thinking probably saved the little girl from serious burns or worse.

Shea fought her way through the panicked crowd, shoving past adults who seemed frozen by shock and terror. She reached the microphone platform and grabbed the device with both hands, her voice cutting through the chaos with practiced authority.

"Everyone move back from the tree! Get away

from the square immediately." Her commands barely penetrated the pandemonium, but some people began moving in the right direction.

The panic continued to spread like wildfire through the crowd. People shoved past one another without consideration, their eyes wide with primal fear and mouths open in silent screams of terror. Parents lost track of children in the melee while elderly residents struggled to move quickly enough to avoid being trampled.

Shea's stomach twisted with sick realization as she surveyed the orchestrated chaos. This wasn't just another arson attack. This was pure theater. The timing, the location, the symbolism of destroying the community's most beloved tradition in front of hundreds of witnesses—everything had been carefully calculated for dramatic effect.

"He specifically wanted this to be seen by as many people as possible," she muttered to Trevor as he returned the rescued child to her grateful mother. "Every scream, every moment of terror, every ounce of fear is part of his twisted performance."

Before Trevor could respond, sirens wailed from somewhere further down Main Street, growing louder as emergency vehicles raced toward some new disaster. Seconds later, Shea's radio crackled to life with another emergency call.

"Sheriff, we have a structure fire at St. Mary's Catholic Church," Doris announced, her normally steady voice shaking with stress. "Father O'Malley is requesting immediate assistance."

"Copy that, we're en route," Shea responded, grateful she'd made the decision to leave Heidi safely at home rather than expose her dog to this dangerous situation. She shouted for Trevor to follow, and they raced down the street toward the historic stone church that had served the community for over a century.

What they found when they arrived made Shea's blood run cold. The elaborate nativity scene that had been St. Mary's pride and joy was completely engulfed in flames, but not from Christmas lights or an electrical malfunction. Someone had deliberately set fire to the display, turning the sacred symbols of hope and peace into a hellish inferno.

The wooden manger, hand-carved by parishioners decades ago, was now a crackling bonfire, with dry straw serving as perfect tinder that spread the flames to every surface. Life-sized statues of Mary and Joseph were blackening rapidly, their carefully painted features melting and running like tears until their faces collapsed into unrecognizable masses of ash and char. The baby Jesus figurine, carved from beautiful cedar and painted with loving detail, was slumping as the resin varnish bubbled and warped, eventually becoming nothing more than a twisted, unidentifiable mass.

The crossbeam that supported the stable's roof groaned under the intense heat, then splintered with a sharp crack that echoed across the churchyard. The entire wooden structure collapsed inward with a crash that sent sparks flying in all directions.

"Daddy, why is Baby Jesus burning?" a small child asked her father, her innocent voice carrying clearly through the night air with heartbreaking confusion.

Father O'Malley, the elderly priest who had served this parish for thirty years, knelt in the snow beside the destroyed nativity. His weathered hands clutched a wooden cross tightly while he whispered desperate prayers through tears that froze on his cheeks in the bitter cold.

Trevor crouched low near the remains of the display, running his gloved fingers carefully across the frost-covered ground. "Accelerant was laid in a perfect straight line from the street to the manger. This fire was painted like a brushstroke—deliberate, artistic, and completely controlled."

"The entire box of donated Christmas gifts is missing," cried Mrs. Patterson, one of the church volunteers who had been coordinating the annual toy drive. "We had presents for over fifty children whose families can't afford Christmas this year. What kind of sick person burns down the nativity and steals gifts meant for kids who won't have a Christmas without them?"

Father O'Malley struggled to his feet, brushing snow from his black cassock with trembling hands. His voice was barely above a whisper but carried the weight of profound grief. "He didn't just burn wood and paint tonight. He burned faith itself—the very foundation of what we believe and what brings us together as a community."

The same young child who had spoken before tugged on her mother's coat sleeve with growing distress. "Mama, if Baby Jesus burned up, does that mean Santa Claus will burn too? "

Her mother had no answer except to pull her daughter close and hold her tight, her own tears falling silently into the child's hair.

By the time Shea and Trevor returned to their vehicles, Main Street was completely deserted except for city workers in reflective safety vests who were already beginning the grim task of sweeping up debris from the destroyed tree. The acrid odor of smoke, melted plastic, and burned dreams hung heavy in the winter air like a toxic cloud that seemed to coat everything it touched.

At the sheriff's station, a pack of reporters had gathered like vultures, their cameras and microphones ready to capture every word. They immediately began firing rapid questions the moment Shea stepped out of her patrol vehicle.

"Sheriff Callahan, does tonight's attack mean you'll be releasing Jake Thompson?"

"Do you have any solid leads on the real perpetrator?"

"What does Mayor Ferguson have to say about these latest incidents?"

"Are you considering requesting assistance from the state police or FBI?"

Before Shea could respond to any of the questions, several cars filled with frightened families pulled into the parking lot. Soon, a crowd of angry and terrified residents had gathered with demands and accusations of their own.

"Our children can't sleep anymore! They're having nightmares every night."

"You arrested that Thompson boy and said the problem was solved! Why isn't this over?"

"If you can't handle this situation, maybe we need to call in the National Guard!"

"How many more attacks before someone gets killed?"

Shea stood on the top step of the building and raised both hands, calling for quiet. The crowd's shouting gradually died down to an expectant murmur. "Yes, Jake Thompson will be released immediately. As we originally determined, he is not the person we're looking for. I'm asking everyone to please go home to your families. Lock your doors and windows. Stay vigilant, but don't let fear control your lives."

She almost added that Christmas was canceled for Misty Hollow that year, but decided against making such a devastating pronouncement in front of news cameras. Instead, she turned and walked into the building, leaving the crowd to disperse on their own.

A middle-aged woman with graying hair and fierce

determination in her eyes stormed through the door immediately behind Shea. "Sheriff, I think you need to take a serious look at Hank Spooner as a suspect. I found a charred Santa suit hidden behind the dumpster in back of his toy store earlier today. I think he might be setting these fires because his business has been failing badly. Everyone orders toys online nowadays instead of shopping at local stores."

"And you are?" Shea narrowed her eyes, studying the woman's face for signs of reliability.

"Betty Wood. I own Wood's Gift Shop right next door to Spooner's Toys. We share a back alley, and I noticed some suspicious activity behind his store this afternoon."

Shea shot a meaningful look at Deputy Butler, who was already reaching for his winter coat. "Bring in Hank Spooner while you're at it."

"I'm on it, Sheriff," he confirmed, rushing toward the door. "I'll check out Mr. Spooner and his store immediately."

As Butler disappeared into the night, Shea slumped into her desk chair and rubbed her temples where a massive headache was building. The arsonist was escalating rapidly, becoming bolder and more theatrical with each attack. The destruction of the town's most sacred symbols—the community Christmas tree and the church nativity—represented a new level that went far beyond simple property damage.

Whoever was behind these attacks wasn't just

trying to destroy buildings or decorations. They were systematically dismantling the very spirit of Christmas in Misty Hollow, targeting the traditions and symbols that brought people together and gave them hope during the darkest time of year.

~

From the shadows beyond the churchyard, concealed behind a cluster of snow-laden pine trees, he stood completely motionless except for the steady rhythm of his breathing. The frost crunched softly under his heavy work boots as he shifted his weight, but the sound was masked by the crackling of dying flames and the distant voices of emergency responders.

He could still feel the intense heat from the burning nativity even from fifty yards away, the warmth touching his face like a caress.

"Do you see them now, Lily?" he whispered to the cold night air, his words forming small clouds that dissipated quickly in the darkness. "They're crying now, just like I cried for you. They're watching their joy burn the same way I watched you burn in our house while nobody came to help us."

He smiled as he observed the children clinging to their parents, their innocent faces streaked with tears of confusion and fear. The sight of Father O'Malley kneeling in the snow, praying over the ruined nativity with desperate grief, filled him with vengeful pleasure. These people were finally beginning to understand what loss felt like, what it meant to watch something precious and irreplaceable turn to ash and memory.

But inside his chest, beneath the satisfaction and triumph, rage still simmered like molten metal. He wasn't finished yet—not even close. Tonight's attacks were just the beginning of his campaign to make Misty Hollow understand the depth of his pain.

"Not enough." His breath formed ghostly wisps in the frigid air. "Not yet. They don't truly know emptiness. They haven't learned what it means to lose everything that matters."

He strolled back toward his hidden vehicle, his footsteps muffled by the snow. "Not until I burn what they love most of all."

The final phase of his plan would come soon. It would be something so devastating, so personally meaningful to every resident of Misty Hollow, that they would never forget Gary Richardson or his sweet Lily ever again.

Chapter Six

"Got it, Sheriff." Deputy Butler dropped a plastic evidence bag on Shea's cluttered desk with a heavy thud. The bag contained what had once been a Santa suit, now nothing more than a grotesque lump of melted synthetic fibers, blackened polyester, and charred fake fur that bore little resemblance to the jolly holiday costume it had once been.

"What about Spooner himself?" Shea asked, eyeing the destroyed costume through the clear plastic. The smell of burned fabric still clung to the evidence bag despite being sealed, a acrid reminder of the night's destruction.

"Sitting in interrogation room two, sweating bullets and looking like he's about to have a heart attack," Butler reported. "Guy's nervous as a long-tailed cat in a room full of rocking chairs."

"Anything else I should know before I question him?"

"Already have a couple of deputies conducting a thorough search of his toy store right now. They should be finished within the next few minutes, and I told them to document everything they find, no matter how insignificant it might seem."

Shea grabbed the evidence bag and headed toward the interrogation rooms, her mind already formulating the questions she needed to ask. As she passed Trevor's desk, where he was typing rapidly on his computer, she paused to check in with him.

"Found anything interesting on Spooner's background?"

Trevor looked up from his screen, his expression grim. "The guy's drowning in debt—three months behind on his mortgage, maxed out credit cards, suppliers threatening to cut him off completely. Money troubles make people do desperate things, but turn someone into a serial arsonist? That doesn't make sense. He wouldn't be getting paid to set these fires, so what would be his motivation?"

Before Shea could respond, Deputy Hudson appeared carrying a large cardboard box that looked like it weighed at least thirty pounds. He set it carefully on the nearest empty desk, breathing heavily from the exertion.

"Sheriff, you're going to want to see this," Hudson announced, wiping sweat from his forehead despite the cold evening. "And there's more evidence coming in from the search, too. The deputies are loading up another vehicle right now."

Shea approached the box and peered inside, immediately recognizing the colorful wrapping paper and neat gift tags that church volunteers had prepared. "Are these the missing Christmas presents from St. Mary's Catholic Church?"

"Every single one of them," Hudson confirmed. "We found boxes of canned food and winter clothing donations as well. All the stuff that was intended for needy families who won't have anything for Christmas without community help."

"Trevor, bring that box with you," Shea ordered, already formulating her interrogation strategy. If Spooner was their arsonist, confronting him with the stolen donations might break his composure and get him to confess.

She marched purposefully to Interrogation Room Two and dropped the evidence bag containing the charred Santa suit on the metal table with deliberate force, the sound echoing off the bare walls. The fluorescent lights overhead cast harsh shadows that made the room feel even more intimidating.

Sweat poured down Hank Spooner's flushed face in steady streams, creating dark stains on his wrinkled dress shirt. The man was overweight, probably in his late fifties, with thinning gray hair and the soft hands of someone who spent his days arranging toy displays rather than engaging in physical labor. This wasn't how she'd pictured their arsonist. The person they were hunting would need to be swift on their feet, physically capable of moving quickly through various terrains, and remain cool under pressure.

Shea took her seat across from Spooner, maintaining steady eye contact while Trevor positioned the box of stolen Christmas gifts directly next to the burned Santa suit. The visual impact of the evidence was exactly what she'd hoped for. Spooner's eyes widened with obvious recognition and guilt.

"Mind explaining how these items were found in and around your store, Mr. Spooner?" Shea kept her voice level and professional, but her tone carried an unmistakable edge of authority.

Before Spooner could respond, Butler quietly entered the room and leaned down to whisper in Shea's ear. "We've got another suspect who was also caught with stolen merchandise. Want me to bring him in?"

"Put him in room one. I'll talk to him as soon as I finish here." She kept her gaze on Spooner. "Now, I'm waiting for an explanation."

Spooner's hands trembled as he folded them on the table in front of him, his wedding ring clicking against the metal surface. "Yeah, okay, I took the stuff from behind the church. Business has been dead for months, and I was desperate for something to sell in my store. But that burned Santa suit isn't mine, and I swear on my mother's grave I didn't set any fires. Why would I destroy property? There's no profit in destruction, Sheriff."

Shea found herself agreeing with his logic, though she kept her expression neutral. "Mr. Spooner, you stole items that were specifically intended for needy children whose families can't afford Christmas presents."

He wiped his sweaty forehead with the back of his sleeve, leaving a damp stain on the fabric. "I'm not proud of what I did. It was wrong, and I know it. But I was facing bankruptcy, losing everything my family had worked for. I doubt anyone will come into my store now anyway, not after word gets out about this mess."

"That's probably an accurate assessment of your situation," Shea agreed, standing from her chair. This man clearly wasn't the sophisticated arsonist they were hunting. He was just another casualty of the economic pressures that had been squeezing small businesses throughout the region. "We'll need to check with Father O'Malley and the church board to see whether they intend to press formal charges. In the meantime, do not leave town, Mr. Spooner. We may have additional questions."

She stepped out of the room where Butler was waiting with a manila folder containing information about their second suspect.

"Vince Jones, local mechanic who lost his job at Patterson's Auto Repair about four months ago," Butler reported, reading from his notes. "Deputies found stolen toys, clothing, and food items hidden throughout his garage. Guy's got two young kids and a wife who's been working double shifts at the diner to make ends meet."

Jones was a stark contrast to the overweight toy store owner. He was rail-thin with prematurely gray hair that looked like it hadn't been cut in months, and his navy work coveralls hung loose on his gaunt frame like clothes borrowed from a much larger man. Dark circles under his eyes spoke of sleepless nights and the kind of stress that consumed a person from the inside.

"I didn't want my kids to wake up on Christmas morning with nothing under the tree," he said before Shea could even sit down. His voice carried the defeated tone of a man who'd reached the end of his options. "They're six and eight years old, Sheriff. They still believe in Santa Claus and the magic of Christmas morning."

"Where exactly did you acquire these items, Mr. Jones?" Shea crossed her arms and leaned against the wall, studying his body language for signs of deception.

"Mostly from unlocked car trunks in parking lots around town," he admitted with obvious shame. "I'd follow shoppers from the stores, wait for them to go into another business, then check if they'd left their vehicles unlocked. One small item at a time, nothing too obvious or expensive. Just enough so my children wouldn't feel forgotten."

"So, you stalked innocent families and stole their Christmas purchases?" Shea frowned, feeling a mix of sympathy and disappointment. The desperation in his voice was genuine, but his actions had violated other families' holiday preparations.

"Yes, ma'am." He hung his head like a scolded child. "I was completely desperate. My unemployment ran out, we're three months behind on rent, and my wife's wages barely cover groceries. I know it was wrong, but I couldn't bear the thought of disappointing my kids."

All she was accomplishing by questioning these two men was wasting precious time that should be spent hunting for the real person responsible for the arsons. Neither Spooner nor Jones had the psychological profile or technical capabilities to plan and execute the sophisticated attacks that had terrorized Misty Hollow.

Shaking her head in frustration, she returned to the main office and handed both suspects over to Butler for processing. Interestingly, despite the thefts from car trunks, no citizens had called the sheriff's department to report missing purchases, which suggested that most people hadn't even noticed the losses yet.

"Mail delivery," announced Doris, the department's longtime receptionist and dispatcher, as she handed Shea a small stack of envelopes that had accumulated during the evening's chaos.

"Thanks, Doris. Any emergency calls while we were dealing with the arrests?"

"Nothing major. A few noise complaints from the apartment complex, and Mrs. Henderson called about suspicious footprints in her backyard again. I told her we'd send someone by in the morning."

Shea flipped through the mail as she walked toward her office, separating official correspondence from what appeared to be community complaints and suggestions from concerned citizens. Most of it could wait until tomorrow, when she had time to focus on administrative tasks.

One envelope immediately caught her attention and stopped her in her tracks. It was a plain white business envelope with her name scrawled across the front in uneven black lettering, along with the correct address for the sheriff's office. No return address, no postmark indicating it had gone through the postal system. Someone had delivered this personally.

She sat heavily at her desk and carefully slid her finger under the envelope's sealed flap, trying to preserve any potential fingerprint evidence. The paper tore with a sound that seemed unnaturally loud in the relative silence of the late evening office.

Inside was a single card made from cheap cardstock, the kind sold in discount stores. Printed across the white surface in uneven strokes with what appeared to be a black marker was a simple but chilling message: "You can't stop the fire. Not after what happened to me."

No signature, no additional explanation, but the implication was crystal clear. This wasn't a random threat from an angry citizen or a prank from bored teenagers. This was direct communication from their arsonist, and she now knew with absolute certainty that the man they were hunting was Gary Richardson—a father who had suffered an unimaginable loss and apparently blamed the entire community for his daughter's death.

She stared at the words until they seemed to swim on the page, her mind racing through the implications of receiving direct contact from the perpetrator. The room suddenly felt cooler despite the building's heating system, and the constant hum of the fluorescent overhead lights seemed to grow louder and more oppressive. Her chest tightened with the uncomfortable realization that she had now become a specific target rather than simply the law enforcement officer trying to catch him.

Trevor entered her office carrying two steaming cups of coffee in ceramic mugs, a routine they'd established during long nights of investigation. He took one look at her face and immediately set both cups down on her desk.

"What's wrong, Shea? You look like you've seen a ghost."

Without saying a word, she slid the card across the desk toward him, watching his expression change as he read the threatening message.

Trevor frowned deeply as he examined the cheap cardstock and crude lettering. "This could be someone trying to stir up trouble, maybe a prank from a teenager who thinks this is all some kind of game."

"No," Shea said with absolute conviction, shaking her head. "This isn't a prank or a false alarm. He's communicating directly with me now, Trevor. Gary Richardson is talking to me."

"Listen, you've been carrying the weight of this entire town's safety on your shoulders for weeks." Trevor settled into the chair across from her desk. "Don't let him get inside your head. That's exactly what he wants—to make you doubt yourself and feel personally responsible for his actions."

Shea leaned back in her chair, feeling the full weight of exhaustion and stress that had been building since the first fire. "He's already inside my head. The moment he decided to target our community's Christmas traditions, he made this personal for everyone involved."

She carefully placed the threatening card into a clear evidence bag, handling it with the same precision she'd use for any crucial piece of evidence. The forensics lab might be able to lift fingerprints or identify the specific type of marker used, though she doubted Richardson had been careless enough to leave evident traces.

Outside the sheriff's office, the December wind whistled through the bare branches of the old oak trees that lined Main Street. The sound carried an almost musical quality that, under different circumstances, might have been pleasant. Tonight, however, it sounded eerily like distant laughter. Cold, mocking, and filled with malevolent amusement.

As Shea listened to the wind's haunting melody, she couldn't shake the feeling that Gary Richardson was out there in the darkness, watching and waiting for the perfect moment to deliver his final, devastating blow against the community that he believed had failed him and his beloved daughter.

The question wasn't whether he would strike again—it was when, where, and how many innocent people might be caught in the crossfire of his quest for revenge against Misty Hollow.

84

Chapter Seven

Shea's radio crackled to life at four in the morning, dragging her from the restless sleep that had become her nightly routine. Dreams of burning buildings and faceless arsonists had haunted her for hours, leaving her tangled in sweat-dampened sheets and fighting the urge to check every lock in her house twice.

"Sheriff Callahan," she answered groggily, already reaching for the clothes she'd laid out the night before—a habit developed from years of emergency calls that couldn't wait for proper preparation.

"We've got a major structure fire on Ash Street," Doris reported, her usually steady voice carrying an edge of urgency that cut through Shea's mental fog. "The old textile mill. Flames are visible from downtown, and we've got reports of someone potentially trapped inside."

After confirming she was en route, Shea sent

Trevor a quick text message letting him know she'd pick him up on her way to the scene. She threw on jeans, boots, and her heavy winter coat.

"You stay here, Heidi," she commanded as the German Shepherd lifted her head hopefully from her bed beside the fireplace. "This one sounds too dangerous, and I need you safe."

The dog whined in protest and flopped back onto her cushion with the resigned sigh of an animal who understood that some adventures were off-limits.

When Shea pulled into Trevor's driveway, he was already waiting on his front porch with a travel mug of coffee and his emergency kit. The partnership they'd developed over months of working together meant they could respond to crises with minimal communication, each anticipating what the other needed.

"How bad is it?" Trevor climbed into the passenger seat, immediately buckling his seatbelt and adjusting the radio to monitor emergency frequencies.

"Bad enough that half the town probably saw the glow from their bedroom windows," Shea replied, pressing harder on the accelerator as they left the residential area and headed toward the industrial district where the old mill stood like a forgotten monument to Misty Hollow's more prosperous past.

When they arrived at the scene, the sky above Ash Street glowed an ominous orange that painted the surrounding buildings in hellish light. The textile mill— a long-forgotten husk of brick and timber that city planners had been promising to demolish for over a decade—was completely engulfed in flames that roared through broken windows like the mouth of an industrial furnace.

The structure had been built in the 1940s to process cotton and wool for military uniforms during World War II, but had been abandoned since the 1980s when manufacturing moved overseas. What remained was a maze of rotting wooden floors, exposed electrical wiring, and debris that created perfect conditions for a catastrophic fire.

Water streamed from multiple fire hoses, but much of it was turning to ice the moment it hit the cracked pavement, creating a treacherous skating rink that made the firefighters' job even more dangerous. Thick smoke rolled across the street in heavy, acrid clouds that burned the eyes and throat, carrying the stench of burning chemicals, old wood, and something else—something organic that made Shea's stomach clench with dread.

Fire Chief Martinez approached them with soot-streaked face and exhaustion etched in every line of his weathered features. "We've got one casualty," he reported grimly. "Body's already been recovered, but it's not pretty."

Three firefighters were carefully maneuvering a stretcher toward the waiting ambulance, their movements slow and respectful despite the chaos surrounding them. A paramedic knelt beside the body, checking for vital signs they all knew wouldn't be there, then shook his head with the finality that confirmed everyone's worst fears.

A charred boot stuck out from under the white sheet, the rubber sole completely melted and fused together at the toes. The sight hit Shea like a physical blow, forcing her to confront the reality that their arsonist had finally crossed the line from property destruction to murder.

"He'd been living in there for months," one of the firefighters explained as he pulled off his helmet and wiped sweat from his forehead despite the frigid morning air. "Tommy Garrett, a local homeless guy who never hurt anybody, just looked for warm places to sleep when the temperature dropped. Old-timers remember him from when he worked at the hardware store before his drinking got bad."

Shea forced herself to approach the stretcher, kneeling briefly beside the covered form despite every instinct telling her to look away. She needed to see this, needed to honor Tommy as more than just another casualty statistic. His burned hands were visible at the edge of the sheet, fingers clutched and contorted as if he'd been reaching desperately for a door handle that wouldn't turn.

"Same accelerant pattern, same technique." Trevor shone his powerful flashlight at the mill's main entrance. "But this time, our arsonist wanted someone to die. Look at this—the door was barred from the outside with a two-by-four. Tommy never had a chance to escape."

The implication sent ice through Shea's veins. This wasn't an accidental death resulting from reckless arson. This was premeditated murder disguised as property destruction. Gary Richardson had deliberately trapped an innocent man inside a burning building, escalating to cold-blooded killing.

She studied the scene with new eyes, noting details that painted a picture of calculated malice. The accelerant had been poured in specific patterns designed to cut off escape routes. This wasn't the work of someone consumed by grief and rage. This was methodical execution.

"We need to evacuate the downtown area," Shea decided. "If he's willing to kill one person, he won't hesitate to take more lives. This changes everything."

~

Gary Richardson stood motionless across the street from the burning mill, his face hidden deep within the shadows of his heavy hood. He blended seamlessly into the small crowd of curious onlookers who had gathered despite the early hour, drawn by the orange glow and distant sirens like moths to a deadly flame.

He watched with cold satisfaction as the stretcher was loaded into the back of the ambulance with careful, respectful movements. No sirens wailed as the vehicle pulled away. There was no need for emergency lights when the passenger was already beyond help. The absence of urgency spoke volumes about Tommy Garrett's fate.

One life extinguished. A nobody that society had forgotten long before the flames claimed him. The bitter irony wasn't lost on Gary. Now they would mourn Tommy, hold vigils and speak of tragedy, though none of them had noticed him sleeping in doorways or offered help when he shivered through winter nights with nothing but cardboard for warmth.

No home, no family, no one who would truly miss him except as a symbol of their own guilt. Just another puff of smoke disappearing into the wind, forgotten as quickly as the ashes would be swept away. They cared more about this homeless drunk than they had ever cared about Gary Richardson or his precious Lily, but their hypocrisy only strengthened his resolve.

This was just the beginning of their education in loss. They hadn't suffered nearly enough to understand the depth of his pain, hadn't lost anything that truly mattered to their comfortable, insulated lives. Tommy Garrett was merely the opening note in a symphony of destruction that would crescendo on Christmas morning.

He turned away from the scene as firefighters continued their futile battle against the inferno, feeling the warmth of the flames against his back like the approval of some ancient god of vengeance. To the emergency responders and worried residents, the fire represented destruction and tragedy. To Gary Richardson, the flames were justice incarnate—beautiful, purifying, and necessary.

The final phase of his plan was already in motion. Soon, Misty Hollow would understand what it meant to lose everything that brought meaning to their lives, just as he had lost Lily in flames that no one had tried to prevent.

~

After eighteen hours of crime scene investigation, witness interviews, and coordinating with state fire marshals, Shea finally returned to her small house on the outskirts of town. The sun was setting behind the mountains, painting the sky in shades of red and gold that reminded her uncomfortably of the morning's fire.

She was surprised to see Trevor's familiar pickup truck already parked in her driveway, but the sight brought a wave of relief rather than annoyance. The truck bed contained a bundled spruce tree dusted with fresh snow, its branches tied carefully with rope to prevent damage during transport.

Trevor was already lifting the six-foot tree onto his broad shoulder as she climbed the front porch steps, her boots crunching on ice that had formed from the afternoon's brief snow shower.

"Don't even think about arguing with me," he said before she could speak, his breath forming small clouds in the cold air. "You need this more than you realize."

Shea's first instinct was to snap at him, to explain

that she didn't have time for holiday nonsense while a murderer stalked their community. But something in Trevor's eyes, a mixture of concern and stubborn determination, stopped the harsh words before they could form.

She unlocked her front door without protesting and stepped aside to let him carry the tree into her living room. Heidi bounded over to investigate the new arrival, her tail wagging as she sniffed the fresh pine scent that now filled the house.

"The boxes of decorations are stored in the spare room closet." Shea hung her coat on the hook by the door. "I'll open a bottle of wine. We both could use something to help us process what we saw today."

When she returned from the kitchen carrying two glasses of red wine, Trevor had already located her modest collection of Christmas decorations and spread them carefully across the sofa. The sight of her meager holiday supplies laid out in the lamplight brought unexpected emotion bubbling to the surface.

Mismatched ornaments collected over the years. Some gifts from colleagues, others purchased on impulse during better times. A few faded red baubles that had belonged to her grandmother. A ceramic angel with a chipped wing that somehow made it more endearing rather than less beautiful. And there, nestled in tissue paper like a precious relic, was a wooden star made from popsicle sticks and painted with childish enthusiasm during her first-grade Christmas craft project.

"These are all I have left from my childhood holidays." She lifted the crude star and remembered the excitement of presenting it to parents who had praised her artistic efforts with genuine enthusiasm.

Trevor reached into his coat pocket and withdrew two small objects wrapped in faded blue tissue. "My mother carved these by hand." He unwrapped wooden stars that showed the skill of someone who had worked with carving tools for decades. "She made one every Christmas until she passed away five years ago. I figured they shouldn't spend another year hidden away in a drawer."

Together, they began the ritual of decorating the tree with movements that were both careful and surprisingly intimate. They strung garland around the branches, hung ornaments with deliberate spacing, and draped tinsel with the attention to detail that transformed a simple evergreen into something magical.

Their hands brushed when they both reached for the same ornament, sending an electric shock up Shea's arm that had nothing to do with static electricity. She didn't pull away from the contact, instead allowing her fingers to linger against his for a heartbeat longer than necessary.

When she stretched to reach a high branch, Trevor steadied her with a gentle hand on her waist. She leaned into his touch for the briefest moment, feeling solid and warm against the uncertainty that had consumed her life for weeks.

They both laughed—a sound that seemed oddly out of place after days of destruction and death—when a string of garland slipped loose and draped itself around Heidi's neck like an improvised collar. The German Shepherd sat patiently while they untangled her, as if she understood that this moment of lightness was precious and shouldn't be disturbed.

At last, Trevor crouched beside the wall outlet with his hand on the light cord, ready to illuminate their handiwork. "You ready to see how it looks?"

Shea shot out her hand to stop him, the motion driven by fears she couldn't fully articulate. "No. Not this year. No lights."

Trevor studied her face for a long moment, reading the anxiety and trauma that she tried so hard to keep hidden from everyone else. Slowly, he released the cord and straightened. "All right. No lights then."

The tree stood in the corner of her living room, decorated but unilluminated, glowing only in the warm light from her fireplace. It was beautiful in its own way, but undeniably dark. A perfect reflection of Misty Hollow itself. Dressed for Christmas but stripped of the joy that should have made the season bright.

They settled side by side on the couch with their wine glasses, the decorated but unlit tree looming in the corner like a monument to complicated emotions. The house felt warmer with Trevor's presence, more like a home than the safe refuge she'd been using to escape from the pressures of her job.

"We'll catch him, Shea," Trevor said quietly, his voice carrying conviction that she desperately wanted to share. "Before he takes another innocent life. Before he completely steals Christmas from this town and everyone who calls it home."

She exhaled slowly, staring at the darkened tree and thinking about Tommy Garrett's final moments trapped in a burning building with no hope of rescue. "I hope you're right, Trevor. I really do."

For a heartbeat that stretched into something more meaningful, their shoulders touched as they sat together in the firelight. His hand brushed hers where it rested on the couch cushion, and neither of them moved away from the contact.

For just a little while, surrounded by the scent of pine and the warmth of flickering flames, she could set aside the weight of responsibility and simply exist in this moment with someone who understood the burden she carried.

Chapter Eight

Shea took a slow sip from the thermos of hot coffee, savoring the warmth as it spread through her chest on another frigid December night. She handed the metal container to Trevor, their fingers brushing briefly in the exchange—a moment of human contact that felt precious after hours of silent surveillance in their unmarked patrol car.

"Stakeouts have to be one of the most mind-numbing aspects of our job," Shea murmured, stretching her neck to work out the kinks that had developed from sitting in the same position for nearly four hours. They'd been parked across from the downtown business district since ten PM, watching for any sign of suspicious activity that might indicate their arsonist was preparing to strike again.

"You think so?" Trevor arched a brow, a slight smile playing at the corners of his mouth despite their grim circumstances. "I actually enjoy them. There's something about the anticipation of seeing—"

The police radio suddenly crackled to life with urgent static that cut through Trevor's words like a blade. Both officers snapped to attention, their casual conversation forgotten as the dispatch coordinator's voice filled the car with the information they'd been waiting weeks to hear.

"All units, we have an anonymous caller reporting a male suspect with multiple gas containers behind Murphy's Mercantile," she reported with professional efficiency. "Suspect appears to be working on some kind of device. Store has been closed for three hours."

Shea snapped upright in the passenger seat, adrenaline instantly sharpening her focus and washing away the fatigue that had been creeping in after days of eighteen-hour shifts. Her heart rate spiked as the implications hit her. This could finally be their chance to catch Gary Richardson in the act.

"That's him," she said with absolute conviction, already reaching for her service weapon to check that it was secure in its holster. "This is our break, Trevor."

"Let's go get him." Trevor started the engine and shifted into drive. He activated the emergency lights but kept the siren silent, not wanting to alert their suspect that law enforcement was closing in on his position.

Murphy's Mercantile loomed ahead of them like a sleeping giant, its weathered brick facade dating back to the 1920s when it had served as the town's primary general store. The front window was painted with

"Merry Christmas" in cheerful red and green letters that seemed mockingly festive given their current mission, and holiday lights sagged around the roofline like drooping eyebrows. The decorative bulbs remained unplugged, swaying gently in the icy wind that had been building throughout the evening.

Behind the main building, delivery pallets and large dumpsters formed a maze of shadows that provided perfect cover for someone who didn't want to be seen. The loading dock was poorly lit, with only a single security light casting weak illumination across the cracked asphalt where delivery trucks normally parked during business hours.

Trevor killed the engine and headlights about fifty yards from the building, positioning their patrol car behind a cluster of bare oak trees that would provide concealment while still allowing them a clear view of the suspect's likely escape routes. They sat in the gathering darkness, watching their breath fog the windows as frost began creeping across the windshield .

A plastic Santa Claus mounted on the store's roof squeaked rhythmically as its mechanical arm waved endlessly into the night, the cheerful gesture made eerily persistent by a motor that probably hadn't been serviced in years. The sound was barely audible over the wind, but somehow made the entire scene feel more surreal and threatening.

"If I were planning an arson attack," Trevor muttered, scanning the area with practiced eyes, "I think I'd pick someplace quieter than the middle of downtown. Too many potential witnesses, too many ways for things to go wrong."

"Murphy's store is like a buffet for someone with his needs." Shea lifted binoculars to get a better view of the loading area. "Fuel, tools, batteries, electrical supplies—everything he needs to construct his incendiary devices and feed his obsession with fire. Plus, it's a local institution. Burning it down would send another message to the community."

Through the binoculars, she could make out a hooded figure crouched near the wooden pallets, methodically dragging what appeared to be a large duffel bag across the frozen ground. The person moved with purpose and familiarity, suggesting this wasn't their first time preparing for such an attack. He set down two distinctive red gasoline containers, then pulled electronic components from the bag—wires, a small rectangular box that looked like a timer, and other items she couldn't identify from this distance.

"Timer device." Trevor squinted through the darkness. "Same methodology as the previous attacks. He's definitely our guy."

Shea lowered the binoculars as her pulse quickened with anticipation and anxiety. "We move in slow and steady. You take the left approach through the parking area, and I'll cut right through the alley. Keep your weapons low until we can positively confirm he's armed and dangerous."

They exited their patrol car with practiced silence, leaving the doors slightly ajar to avoid the distinctive sound of metal latching that might alert their suspect. Moving with the coordinated precision they'd developed through months of working together, they crept forward across the frost-covered ground, their boots crunching softly over ice crystals that sparkled in the weak streetlight.

The suspect remained completely absorbed in his work, apparently oblivious to their careful approach. Shea could see him more clearly now. Tall and broad-shouldered, wearing dark clothing and moving with the confidence of someone who had done this many times before. His hands worked quickly and efficiently with the electronic components, suggesting technical knowledge that matched their profile of Gary Richardson.

A sudden gust of wind blew an empty aluminum can across the asphalt, the metallic scraping sound unnaturally loud in the quiet night. The suspect's head jerked up, his body going rigid as he scanned the area for the source of the noise. For a heartbeat that seemed to stretch into eternity, he remained perfectly still, like a deer sensing danger in the forest.

Then, without warning, he abandoned his materials and bolted into the maze of shadows between the buildings.

"Cut him off!" Trevor abandoned stealth as he sprinted toward the loading dock area where their suspect had disappeared.

Shea veered right as planned, her heart pounding with excitement and determination as she wove through narrow alleys lined with dumpsters, stacked shipping crates, and the detritus of small-town commerce. This was their chance, possibly their only chance, to end the reign of terror that had gripped Misty Hollow for weeks.

The suspect was incredibly fast, his feet slapping against the slick pavement with the rhythm of someone in excellent physical condition. His dark hood flapped behind him like a banner as he darted through gaps between buildings that seemed almost too narrow for a person to navigate, yet he moved through them with the fluid grace of someone intimately familiar with these back alleys.

Shea caught a quick glimpse of his profile as he passed under a streetlight. Shadowed and indistinct, but tall and broad-shouldered just as the witnesses had described. The image lodged itself in her memory like a photograph, though she couldn't make out enough detail to provide a useful description to other officers.

She rounded the corner of Murphy's Hardware Store at full sprint, expecting to see the suspect cornered or at least visible in the narrow alley that dead-ended against the back of the pharmacy. Instead, she found nothing but emptiness and two abandoned fuel cans sitting beside a rusted dumpster, a scattered tangle of electronic wires, and the lingering scent of gasoline that confirmed this had been their arsonist's staging area.

"How could I have lost him?" Her chest heaved from the exertion and frustration. "He was right here just seconds ago."

Trevor appeared moments later, equally winded and clearly disappointed by their failure to apprehend their primary suspect. "It's like we're chasing smoke." He shook his head and holstered his service weapon. "Every time we get close, he just vanishes into thin air."

"There has to be an explanation." She studied the alley for clues they might have missed. "People don't just disappear. He's using these back streets and alleys like a highway system, moving through routes he's probably practiced dozens of times."

Trevor leaned against the brick wall of the pharmacy, his breath forming small clouds in the cold air. "We need rest, Shea. We're both exhausted, running on adrenaline and coffee, and we're not thinking clearly. We'll never catch him if we aren't operating at one hundred percent capacity."

"I don't have the luxury of slowing down or taking breaks," she snapped back, frustration and exhaustion making her voice sharper than she intended. "Every night that we fail to catch him, another building burns. Another family loses their home, their business, their sense of security. And now he's graduated to murder."

Trevor's voice hardened with a determination she

rarely heard from him. "Then we stop sitting around waiting for him to make a mistake and actually set a trap. This reactive approach isn't working. He's always one step ahead because he chooses the time and place for every encounter. We need to force him into a situation where we control the variables."

Shea spun to face him. "I'm not gambling with innocent people's lives. If our trap fails, if we miscalculate or underestimate him, civilians could die. Look what happened to Tommy Garrett when we weren't there to protect him."

They stood less than three feet apart in the narrow alley, their breath clouding the winter air as tension crackled between them like electricity. The argument carried undercurrents of weeks of stress, sleepless nights, and the growing attraction they'd both been trying to ignore amid the crisis consuming their community.

Trevor's expression softened slightly, and when he spoke again, his voice carried a vulnerability that caught her off guard. "I don't want to lose you, Shea. Not to this job, not to the stress, and especially not to him. If we don't catch Gary Richardson soon, he's going to escalate again. And next time, he might target you personally."

"No, he won't," she replied automatically, but even as she spoke the words, her mind was racing through the implications of the threatening note she'd received. The truth was that Gary Richardson had already made this personal by communicating directly with her. But if she admitted that fear aloud, Trevor might insist on protective custody or other measures that would interfere with her ability to do her job.

More troubling was the growing realization that Richardson might target Trevor as a way to get to her. The thought of losing her partner, both professionally and personally, to the arsonist's twisted campaign of revenge was almost unbearable.

Her radio suddenly burst with static, cutting through the tension like a knife. "Sheriff Callahan, we've got another structure fire downtown," Dispatch reported with barely controlled urgency. "Corner of Main and Third Street. Fire department is en route."

Shea and Trevor exchanged a look that communicated volumes without words—frustration, determination, and the shared understanding that their work was far from over. They sprinted back to their patrol car, knowing that while they'd been chasing shadows in the alleys behind Murphy's Mercantile, Gary Richardson had been implementing the next phase of his plan somewhere else entirely.

There would be no rest for either of them tonight, and possibly not for many nights to come. The arsonist was escalating his attacks, becoming bolder and more frequent in his strikes against the community. They were running out of time to stop him before he claimed more innocent lives in his twisted quest for revenge against Misty Hollow.

~

Pressed against the weathered brick wall of Misty Hollow's Drugstore, Gary Richardson leaned heavily against the cold surface as his lungs burned from the desperate sprint through the maze of downtown alleyways. Despite the physical discomfort and the near-miss with capture, his smile never faded from his weathered face. If anything, the close encounter had energized him, confirming that he was still smarter and more resourceful than the law enforcement officers trying to hunt him down.

He could hear them clearly in the distance—heavy boots pounding against pavement, radios crackling with urgent communications, Sheriff Callahan's sharp voice cutting through the night air as she coordinated the search effort. They were close, uncomfortably close to catching him in the act. And yet, like every previous encounter, they would ultimately go home empty-handed while he remained free to continue his campaign of justice against the town that had failed him and his beloved Lily.

Through a crack in the drugstore's back door, a gap he'd discovered weeks ago during his reconnaissance of potential escape routes, he could observe the two officers as they stood in the alley where he'd been working just minutes before. They were silhouetted against the glow of their patrol car's headlights, their body language revealing frustration and exhaustion that he found deeply satisfying.

Sheriff Callahan's shoulders were rigid with tension, her jaw set tight with barely controlled fury. Trevor leaned toward her with words that were too low for Gary to overhear, but their intimate positioning suggested a relationship that went beyond mere professional partnership.

She was running herself ragged chasing shadows and pursuing leads that led nowhere, exactly as he had intended. The beautiful irony was that her dedication to catching him was destroying her both physically and emotionally, creating the same kind of desperate exhaustion he'd felt during Lily's final weeks when mounting bills and failing health had consumed every moment of his existence.

But Sheriff Callahan still didn't see the bigger picture developing around her. Not yet. She was focused on individual fires, specific locations, tactical responses to his attacks. She hadn't grasped that each incident was part of a larger symphony of destruction designed to culminate in the most devastating strike of all.

His gaze lingered on her as she stood in the alley, noting how the stress had carved new lines around her eyes and the way her hand never strayed far from her service weapon. She was the one he specifically wanted watching when his masterpiece unfolded. She had to see it burn with her own eyes, had to understand that her failure to catch him had allowed the ultimate tragedy to occur.

When her radio crackled with news of the fire he'd set earlier that evening, a carefully timed distraction designed to draw emergency responders away from the Murphy's Mercantile area while he made his preparations, Gary slipped quietly from the doorway and melted back into the network of shadows that had become his highway through Misty Hollow.

The cold December night swallowed him completely, leaving behind only the faint scent of gasoline clinging to his clothes and the satisfaction of knowing that Christmas morning would bring Sheriff Callahan a gift she would never forget.

Chapter Nine

The old, stone community hall smoldered in the pale dawn light, its century-old structure reduced to a skeletal shadow of the gathering place that had served Misty Hollow for generations. The roof had collapsed completely inward during the night, leaving behind sagging rock walls that looked like broken teeth against the gray December sky. Steam rose from the wreckage where snow melted on contact with surfaces still radiating heat, and fire department hoses continued to spray water over hot spots that refused to die. The acrid stink of burned insulation, charred wood, and melted plastic clung to the frigid air like a toxic fog.

Sheriff Shea Callahan stood at the edge of the debris field, her winter gloves already blackened from soot and ash. She'd been sifting through the destruction for over an hour, methodically working her way from the perimeter toward what had once been the main entrance. Every careful movement sent up small clouds of gray powder that coated her uniform and settled in her hair like premature aging.

The community hall had been scheduled to host the annual children's Christmas pageant in just three days. The same event that had been the pride of Misty Hollow for over seventy years. Costumes had been stored in the back room, sets had been constructed by volunteer parents, and programs had already been printed. Now it was all gone, consumed by Gary Richardson's relentless campaign to destroy everything that brought joy to the community during the holiday season.

Shea's flashlight beam cut through the dim morning light, sweeping across mounds of debris that had once been stage curtains, wooden benches, and holiday decorations. Something caught her eye—a faint glimmer barely visible beneath layers of ash and charred fabric. She knelt carefully, her knees sinking into the still-warm rubble, and began brushing aside the debris with her gloved hands.

Her fingers closed around a small, twisted shape that felt both delicate and solid at the same time. She lifted it carefully from its burial place, turning it slowly in the beam of her flashlight. It was a locket, melted and warped by intense heat, but still intact enough that a faint engraving showed through the damage. She angled it toward better light, squinting at the letters that had been etched into the gold surface before fire had tried to erase them.

L.G.

Her throat tightened painfully as recognition flooded through her. Lily Garrison. The little girl who had died in the house fire last Christmas, the tragedy that had transformed Gary Richardson from a struggling father into a vengeful arsonist. For a long beat, Shea couldn't move, couldn't breathe, just stared at the damaged locket as if it might burn her hand the way fire had consumed its original owner.

This wasn't random debris from the fire. This was a message, a calling card, a piece of evidence deliberately left for law enforcement to find. Gary Richardson was telling them exactly who he was and why he was doing this, leaving breadcrumbs of his daughter's memory scattered across the ruins of community tradition.

Deputy Trevor Bolton appeared at her side, his own clothing covered in soot and his face showing the exhaustion of another sleepless night. He knelt beside her in the ash, angling his flashlight low to illuminate the twisted metal in her palm.

"That's no coincidence," he said quietly. "He placed this here deliberately. He wanted us to find it."

"No, it's definitely not a coincidence," Shea agreed, her voice rough from smoke inhalation and emotion. She carefully placed the locket into an evidence bag, sealing it with hands that trembled slightly despite her attempt at professional composure. "But we already know Gary Richardson is behind these fires. We know his motivation, his pattern, his psychological profile. We just haven't been able to catch him. Yet."

The word "yet" carried all her determination and frustration. Weeks of investigation, countless near-misses, and the growing body count that now included Tommy Garrett's senseless death. Every fire brought them closer to understanding Richardson's mind, but understanding wasn't the same as capture.

Hours later, back at the sheriff's office, the case board glowed under harsh fluorescent lights that made everyone look slightly ill. Photographs were arranged in chronological order across the corkboard surface, each one depicting a different location Richardson had targeted. The Miller house. The Stevenson estate. Lucy's Diner. St. Mary's nativity scene. The downtown Christmas tree. The textile mill where Tommy had died. And now, the community hall that had been scheduled to host generations of Christmas memories.

The melted locket in its evidence bag rested in the center of the conference table like an accusation, catching the light and drawing every eye toward it no matter how hard they tried to focus on other aspects of the investigation.

Shea stood before the board with a red marker in hand, her mind working through patterns and connections she'd been too close to see before. She began drawing circles around each photograph, her movements deliberate and precise. When she stepped back to view the whole pattern, the red circles glowed like targets on a map of destruction.

"He's not chasing cheap thrills or looking for attention," she said, speaking partly to Trevor and partly to herself as she worked through the profile. "He's systematically dismantling traditions, targeting the specific things that matter most to this town's identity. One by one, he's erasing what makes Misty Hollow feel like home during Christmas."

Trevor rubbed the back of his neck, a gesture she'd come to recognize as his way of processing stress and exhaustion. "We've known from the beginning that he hates Christmas. The holiday represents everything he lost when Lily died. The joy, innocence, family traditions, hope for the future."

Shea turned from the board and pointed at the locket sitting on the table. "But this isn't just hatred. This is grief manifesting as rage. This is deeply personal pain being externalized as violence against an entire community. Every match he strikes, every fire he sets, is a way to force this town to feel exactly what he felt when Lily burned to death while neighbors watched and did nothing to help him rebuild his life."

The profile was becoming clearer with each piece of evidence. Gary Richardson wasn't simply an arsonist. He was a father trying to make the world understand the magnitude of his loss by destroying the things others loved. If he couldn't have Christmas with his daughter, then no one in Misty Hollow would experience the joy of the season.

Deputy Butler entered the conference room carrying a stack of updated reports from the state fire marshal. "Preliminary analysis confirms the same accelerant and timer mechanism at the community hall. He's not varying his technique because he doesn't need to. It works every time."

"Confidence," Trevor observed. "He's comfortable with his methods and doesn't feel pressure to adapt because we haven't gotten close enough to force a change in strategy."

Shea studied the timeline they'd constructed, looking for gaps or patterns that might predict his next target. "What's left? What hasn't he burned yet that would complete his campaign against Christmas in Misty Hollow?"

The question hung in the air like smoke, unanswered but terrifying in its implications.

~

Earlier that night, Richardson had stood across the street from the community hall, his weathered face hidden deep within the shadows of his heavy hood. The fire he'd set consumed the building, flames racing through dry wood and ancient insulation while wreaths and garland blackened into unrecognizable shapes.

In his right hand, Lily's locket had gleamed faintly in the firelight, its delicate chain brittle from age and the year it had spent in his mountain cabin serving as both memorial and motivation. He'd given it to her for her sixth birthday, watching her face light up with wonder as she opened the small velvet box. She'd worn it every day after that, never taking it off except to sleep.

He could see Lily as clearly as if she stood before him in the snow. Twirling in her red Christmas dress with white lace trim, clutching the locket against her small chest as she prepared to perform in the community hall's annual pageant. She'd been cast as an angel that year, complete with cardboard wings covered in glitter that she'd helped create during craft sessions at the elementary school.

His lungs burned with more than smoke inhalation as he remembered the pure joy radiating from her face during rehearsals. She'd practiced her lines endlessly at home, performing for an audience of one while he sat in their threadbare armchair and applauded every recitation. "Look, Daddy!" she'd called from their makeshift stage. "I'm flying."

Two weeks later, she'd been gone—consumed by flames from a faulty space heater he couldn't afford to replace, dying in a house fire while he'd been outside gathering wood to supplement their inadequate heating. The memory of her screams would haunt him until his own dying day.

As the community hall burned, Gary had knelt in the snow at the edge of the property and pressed the locket deep into the ash near the main entrance. A spot he knew investigators would carefully examine. The metal was warm in his palm, carrying heat from the fire but also from the year it had spent pressed against his own chest, worn on a chain beneath his shirt like a talisman of grief.

"This was yours, Lily," he whispered to the absent ghost of his daughter. "Now it belongs to them. Now they'll see what they stole from us. They'll understand that we mattered, that you mattered, that your life meant something more than a few days of sympathy before everyone moved on with their comfortable lives."

Emergency sirens wailed closer, their distinctive sound cutting through the crackling of burning wood. Red and blue lights painted the smoke in alternating colors as fire trucks and patrol cars converged on the scene. Gary rose slowly from his kneeling position and melted back into the forest that bordered the property, moving along paths he'd scouted weeks earlier for exactly this purpose.

He disappeared into the darkness unseen, a faint smile touching his lips as he imagined Sheriff Callahan discovering the locket and finally understanding the depth of his purpose. The game was entering its final phase, and soon, very soon, Misty Hollow would learn what it truly meant to lose everything on Christmas morning.

~

Late that night, long after other deputies had gone home to steal a few hours of sleep, Shea sat alone in the conference room with only Heidi for company. The German Shepherd slept peacefully under the table, occasionally twitching in her dreams and offering soft whines that suggested she was chasing rabbits through summer fields far removed from the winter nightmare consuming their town.

The evidence board loomed before Shea like an accusation she couldn't answer. She'd been staring at it for over an hour, searching for patterns or connections she'd missed during the daytime chaos of investigation and coordination. Her coffee had gone cold in its mug, untouched for the past thirty minutes.

Richardson couldn't be far. He'd want to be close enough to fulfill his agenda. So, where was he?

She reached across the conference table and pulled the evidence bag containing the locket closer, holding it up to the light and studying the warped metal that had once been a father's gift to his beloved daughter.

"If I'd been sheriff last Christmas, would I have been able to stop it?" she whispered to the empty room, voicing a question that had haunted her since discovering Richardson's identity. "Would I have noticed the dangerous conditions in his house? Would I have connected the community to resources that might have prevented the tragedy?"

The rational part of her mind knew the answer was probably not. She hadn't even been aware of his existence before beginning this investigation, and social services had been stretched too thin to catch every family in crisis. The space heater that sparked and caused Lily's death had been a ticking time bomb that no one could have predicted or prevented.

"But I haven't stopped any of the fires this year either." She gave voice to the guilt that gnawed at her during sleepless nights. "Every morning, I wake up wondering where he'll strike next, and every night I go home knowing I've failed to protect this community one more day."

The guilt was irrational, unsupported by evidence or reasonable expectations of law enforcement capabilities. She wasn't personally responsible for the fire that had killed Lily Garrison, nor was she directly culpable for the child's father's subsequent campaign of arson and murder. But guilt didn't operate on logic. It dug at her consciousness regardless, whispering that a better sheriff would have solved this case weeks ago.

The threatening card she'd received echoed in her head with the persistence of a song she couldn't shake: "You can't stop the fire. Not after what happened to me." Richardson was right about one thing—she hadn't stopped him yet. But he was wrong about her breaking under pressure.

Shea pressed her palms flat against the cold table surface, using the physical sensation to anchor herself in reality. "You want me rattled. You want me broken, consumed by guilt and second-guessing every decision. Not happening. I'm going to catch you, and I'm going to make sure Lily's memory isn't twisted into justification for murder."

She forced herself to look at each photograph on the evidence board again, this time searching not for patterns in his attacks but for vulnerabilities. What was his endgame? Where did this campaign of destruction lead? And most importantly—what was the final target that would complete his revenge against Misty Hollow?

Outside the conference room windows, snow began to fall in thick flakes that promised to blanket the town in fresh white by morning. The scene would have been beautiful under different circumstances, the kind of picture-perfect Christmas card snowfall that Misty Hollow prided itself on during the holiday season.

Shea shut off the conference room lights and called quietly to Heidi, who scrambled to her feet and shook off sleep before padding to her handler's side. Together they walked through the darkened sheriff's office toward the exit, leaving the locket on the table where it would wait until morning to reveal whatever secrets it still held.

As she locked the building and walked toward her truck, Shea couldn't shake the feeling that time was running out. That Richardson's masterpiece was approaching, and she was no closer to stopping it than she'd been the night of the first fire weeks ago.

Chapter Ten

The Fellowship Hall of St. Mary's Catholic Church glowed with warm golden light that spilled through tall, stained-glass windows onto the snow-covered grounds outside. The sound of children's laughter mixed with the adult choir warming up their voices for the evening's special Christmas service, creating a symphony of joy that should have been comforting but instead set Shea's nerves on edge.

A massive Norwegian spruce towered over the spacious room, easily fifteen feet tall and decorated with hundreds of ornaments collected over generations of parish celebrations. The tree glittered with lights, tinsel, and hand-crafted decorations made by Sunday school children, its golden star brushing against the exposed wooden rafters that dated back to the church's construction in 1892. The mingled scents of fresh pine, rich hot cocoa, and spiced cinnamon filled the air with the essence of Christmas tradition.

For a brief moment, it felt like Misty Hollow had reclaimed its Christmas spirit—like Gary Richardson's campaign of terror had failed to break the community's determination to celebrate despite the fear that had gripped them for weeks. But Shea's gut refused to quiet.

She kept scanning the crowded room with the systematic attention of someone expecting an attack, her eyes repeatedly returning to linger on the magnificent spruce tree. It was too perfect, too vulnerable, too symbolic of everything Richardson had been systematically destroying. She shouldn't have allowed this gathering to proceed, shouldn't have let the mayor and Father O'Malley convince her that the community needed this moment of defiance.

Trevor nudged her gently with his elbow, keeping his voice low enough that nearby families wouldn't overhear. "You're twitchier than a long-tailed cat in a room full of rocking chairs. Try to relax, at least a little bit."

"Richardson won't let this pass," Shea whispered back, her hand unconsciously checking her service weapon for the third time in ten minutes. "All these people gathered in one place, celebrating Christmas traditions in a church—it's everything he hates. These people are lambs being led to slaughter, and I allowed them to be brought them here."

Trevor's expression remained calm, but she could see the tension in his jaw. "The entire sheriff's department is here working security, plus half the volunteer fire department. Richardson shouldn't be able to get anywhere near this building without someone spotting him first. We've got two fire trucks positioned outside with crews ready to respond within seconds."

"There's always an outside approach." Her mind raced through the vulnerabilities she'd identified during her security assessment that afternoon. "If a fire starts outside and he manages to bar the doors like he did with Tommy Garrett at the textile mill, it would be the end of everyone in this building. Don't let your guard down for even a second, Trevor."

"Never do." He turned his attention back to the crowd as families began settling into the folding chairs arranged in neat rows facing a small stage where the children's choir would perform.

A few minutes later, the adult choir launched into a beautiful rendition of "Silent Night," their harmonized voices filling the fellowship hall with the kind of pure emotion that made Christmas services memorable. The children's choir waited excitedly off to the side, fidgeting in their matching red and white robes and whispering to each other about who would get to hold the special candles during their performance.

A little boy of perhaps five-years-old tripped over his own feet in his excitement, spilling his cup of hot cocoa in a brown splash that spread across the polished floor near the base of the massive tree. His mother rushed over to comfort him while Shea instinctively moved to help, kneeling down with paper napkins to clean up the spill before someone slipped on the liquid.

As she bent close to the floor, a faint chemical odor rose above the natural scent of pine needles. Something sharp and petroleum-based that didn't belong in a church fellowship hall. Her blood turned to ice as recognition flooded through her.

She crouched lower, pushing aside thick garland to examine the tree's trunk more closely. Her flashlight beam caught on thin copper wires that had been carefully taped along the bark, running up into the dense branches and leading to several small black boxes tucked strategically throughout the tree's interior where they wouldn't be visible to casual observers.

"Oh, dear Lord." Fear threatened to choke her as the full horror of the situation became clear. The entire tree was rigged to explode—not just burn, but detonate in a fireball that would consume everyone in the room within seconds.

She lunged for the microphone at the choir stand, yanking it from the startled choir director's hands. "Everyone out of the building right now! This is an emergency evacuation—move toward the exits immediately!"

The choir broke off mid-note, their beautiful harmony dissolving into confused silence. Parents instinctively scooped up their children, some moving toward the exits while others stood frozen by shock and confusion. Within seconds, panic rippled through the crowd as people realized the sheriff's warning was genuine.

Chairs toppled backward as the congregation surged toward the three exit doors in a wave of desperation. The carefully organized seating arrangement dissolved into chaos as survival instinct overrode social courtesy. Ornaments rained down from the spruce tree like deadly hail, shattering on the tiled floor as panicked bodies bumped against the branches in their desperate flight. Thick garland ripped free from the tree, tangling around people's feet and threatening to trip them. A small child cried out for his mother somewhere in the crush of bodies, his voice barely audible above the growing roar of fear.

Trevor waded directly into the chaos with the calm authority that made him effective in crisis situations. "Slow down, people! No pushing. You'll hurt each other. Keep moving steadily toward the exits." He spotted a little girl being jostled dangerously by the crowd and immediately lifted her onto his broad shoulders to keep her from being trampled, carrying her safely toward the nearest door while calling out directions to confused families.

While Trevor orchestrated the evacuation, Shea's eyes scanned the edges of the crowded room with predatory focus. Where was Richardson? Her finely-tuned instincts screamed that he was present, close by, watching his masterpiece unfold. He wouldn't want to miss this final show—the culmination of his campaign against the community that he blamed for his daughter's death.

From behind the elevated choir risers at the back of the room, a figure stepped slowly into view. Richardson pulled back his hood, revealing a face made hollow by grief and obsession, lit eerily by the multicolored twinkling lights of the tree he'd transformed into a bomb. He held a matchbook in his right hand, his gaze fixed on the spruce with an expression that was almost reverent—like a priest approaching an altar for the most sacred ritual of his faith.

Shea drew her service weapon with practiced speed and aimed it steadily at his center mass. "Gary, don't do this. Please."

His voice carried across the thinning chaos with eerie calm, each word deliberate and weighted with the grief of a year's worth of suffering. "She died choking on smoke while this town sang Christmas carols in warm churches. You honestly think I'll let them laugh and celebrate while I remember her burning? While I remember her screams?"

Despite everything, the fires, the destruction, Tommy Garrett's murder, Shea felt a wave of sympathy for this broken man. She forcibly shoved it down, knowing that compassion couldn't override the need to protect the innocent people still evacuating behind her.

"Lily wouldn't have wanted this," she said, keeping her voice steady and her weapon trained on his chest. "She was a child who loved Christmas. She wanted joy and laughter, not death and destruction. She wouldn't want you to hurt other children in her name."

Richardson's hand trembled violently as he whirled to fully face her, his eyes wild with madness and pain. "Don't you dare speak her name! You have no right. You didn't watch her die. You didn't hear her calling for me while the flames consumed her. You didn't smell her burning."

"I'm deeply sorry for what happened to Lily," Shea said, taking a careful step toward him while maintaining her firing stance. "No child should die that way—no parent should have to endure what you've endured. But no one else needs to die tonight. Please, Gary, put down the matches and let me help you."

Richardson struck a match against the striker strip with deliberate slowness. The flare glowed bright orange, reflecting in his wild eyes as his hood fell back. Time seemed to slow as Shea watched the small flame dance at the end of the wooden stick.

Trevor barreled into Richardson from the side like a linebacker, driving him backward into the base of the massive spruce with enough force to shake more ornaments loose from branches. The lit match tumbled through the air in a graceful arc, then sputtered out harmlessly against the tiled floor as the last panicked members of the congregation fled into the cold night air outside.

Richardson fought with the desperate strength of a

man possessed by demons only he could see, his elbows and fists slamming repeatedly into Trevor's ribs with impacts that would leave brutal bruises. They crashed into the tree again, sending more ornaments exploding against the floor in colorful shards of broken glass and shattered memories.

Shea dove into the violent struggle, grappling for the matchbook still clutched in Gary's left hand. His grip was iron-strong, fingers locked around the cardboard with the determination of someone who had nothing left to lose. She wrenched his wrist backward with all her strength.

He managed to strike another match despite her efforts.

Without hesitation, Shea smothered the flame with her bare palm, pressing her hand directly onto the burning match head. Searing heat scorched her skin, the smell of burning flesh mixing with smoke and pine. She bit back a cry of pain but didn't release her grip on his wrist.

Richardson laughed, a sound devoid of humor or sanity, and spit blood from where Trevor's elbow had connected with his mouth. "Too late, Sheriff. It's already too late to stop it."

He pulled a small electronic detonator from his jacket pocket with his free hand and pressed the red button before either officer could react.

The entire spruce tree ignited in a roaring column of fire that reached the rafters in seconds. The explosion wasn't the massive fireball Shea had feared, but rather a calculated ignition of accelerant-soaked branches designed to trap anyone still inside. The golden star toppled from the top, crashing down in a shower of sparks and burning tinsel. Delicate paper snowflakes that had been strung across the ceiling ignited in cascading waves. Thick garland smoldered and dripped burning synthetic material. The heavy curtains covering the fellowship hall's windows caught fire as flames spread with terrifying speed.

Wooden beams groaned overhead, stressed beyond their century-old capacity by intense heat. The smoke alarm's piercing wail seemed almost comical given the magnitude of the disaster unfolding. Now there were only three people trapped inside, Shea, Trevor, and Richardson, surrounded by growing flames and collapsing architecture.

Trevor coughed violently, while maintaining his hold on Richardson and dragging the arsonist backward by his collar away from the worst of the flames. "We've got maybe thirty seconds before this entire place comes down on top of us."

Shea cradled her burned palm against her chest, feeling the sickening throb of damaged tissue. "We aren't dying here tonight. Not after everything."

Pinned between the two officers, Richardson continued to laugh with the hollow sound of someone who had already surrendered to death. "You can't stop it, Sheriff. I told you from the beginning that you can't stop the fire. It consumes everything eventually."

A burning support beam crashed down from the ceiling, landing less than six feet from where they struggled. Embers scattered across the floor.

Shea's eyes streamed with tears from the blinding smoke, her vision reduced to vague shapes backlit by orange flames. Her uniform stuck to her skin with sweat and soot, the fabric beginning to smoke from radiant heat. Every breath felt like inhaling broken glass.

"We don't have long," Trevor's voice came out as a harsh rasp as he continued wrestling with Richardson, who seemed determined to drag them all into the flames with him.

"This is where it ends!" Richardson screamed above the roar of fire. "Fire takes everything. It took Lily, and now it takes Misty Hollow."

Shea pressed her service weapon firmly to his temple, her finger on the trigger. "Not today, Gary."

With a desperate surge of strength fueled by madness and grief, Richardson shoved them both backward and lunged toward the flaming tree as if to embrace it like a lover. "For Lily! This is all for you, sweetheart."

Trevor wrapped both arms around the crazed man's waist and used his weight to force Richardson backward toward the nearest exit before the man could catch fire. Already, his clothes burned. The door they'd planned to use was now completely engulfed in flames, blocking their primary escape route.

For a brief second, Shea seriously considered letting Richardson burn, simply releasing him to face the fate he'd dealt to so many buildings and to Tommy Garrett. Her jaw clenched with the moral weight of the decision. Instead, duty and conscience won out over vengeance. She grabbed Richardson's arm and helped Trevor drag the screaming, thrashing man toward a large stained-glass window depicting the nativity scene. The window had already cracked from the intense heat, its lead channels beginning to melt.

She kicked the weakened window with every ounce of strength she had left, her lungs wheezing desperately for oxygen. The beautiful glass exploded outward in a shower of colored fragments, and a blessed cold wind rushed into the superheated room like salvation itself.

Trevor shoved Richardson through the broken window frame first, the arsonist's body tumbling onto the snow-covered ground outside. Shea dove after him, rolling across razor-sharp shards of broken glass with her burned hand pressed protectively against her chest. Trevor leaped out last as the fellowship hall's roof caved inward behind them with a thunderous roar that shook the frozen ground.

Firefighter hoses from the two waiting trucks did nothing to stop the inferno consuming St. Mary's. The building was lost before they could even begin a meaningful response.

Members of the parish and rescued congregation

members cried openly as they watched in horror while a church that had served Misty Hollow for over a century was reduced to rubble and ash. Generations of baptisms, weddings, funerals, and Christmas celebrations disappeared into smoke.

Deputies Butler and Hudson rushed forward to handcuff Richardson, hauling him roughly to his feet. His eyes still gleamed with wild satisfaction despite his capture, as if destroying the church had made everything worthwhile.

Trevor staggered against a fire truck, coughing so hard his entire body shook. Shea slumped down beside him, digging frantically in her jacket pocket for the emergency inhaler she carried for situations exactly like this, her asthma exacerbated by smoke inhalation.

"We did it," Trevor managed to say between coughs, his voice barely recognizable.

She nodded, taking a desperate puff from the inhaler, holding it in her lungs, then taking another. The medication began opening her constricted airways almost immediately. "Richardson will spend the rest of his life in prison, reliving the fact that he failed to kill anyone tonight. That thought should have brought me satisfaction, but it doesn't."

Her gaze met Trevor's through the smoke and falling snow. The bond between them, forged in literal flames over weeks of crisis, was louder and more meaningful than any words they could speak. They'd survived Gary Richardson's final revenge, but the scars, both physical and mental, would remain long after the ashes cooled.

Chapter Eleven

Snow fell in thick, wet flakes that melted the moment they touched the steaming rubble of St. Mary's fellowship hall. The moisture in the air created a strange fog that hung over the destruction like a shroud, illuminated by emergency lights from vehicles that had been parked around the perimeter for hours. Fire trucks idled with engines running to keep equipment from freezing, their pulsing red lights painting the ancient stone church in alternating waves of crimson and shadow.

The magnificent spruce tree that had towered inside the fellowship hall was gone, collapsed into a blackened skeleton that still hissed with embers despite the gallons of water firefighters had poured over it. The golden star that had brushed the rafters lay twisted beyond recognition in the rubble, its light extinguished forever.

Deputies Butler and Hudson wrestled Gary

Richardson across the snow-covered ground toward a waiting ambulance, their grips firm on his arms despite his violent resistance. His burned coat hung in charred tatters, revealing blistered skin beneath. His hair was singed down to the scalp in places, and his face showed the raw, weeping burns of someone who'd gotten too close to his own inferno.

Still, he fought against their restraint with the desperate strength of madness, coughing black soot into the cold night air. His laughter came out jagged and sharp as broken glass, the sound of a mind that had shattered long before his body suffered its injuries.

"She burned, Sheriff!" he rasped, twisting his body toward Shea with wild eyes that reflected the dying embers behind them. His voice carried the ragged quality of vocal cords damaged by smoke inhalation. "She burned while this town did nothing, and now you'll all burn in your memories just like I do every single night."

Shea stood apart from the scene, her bandaged hand pressed protectively against her chest where the pain throbbed with her elevated heartbeat. She said nothing in response to his accusations. She didn't feel triumph, but instead, the hollow aftermath of survival. Her silence hit Richardson harder than any words could have, a verdict delivered without need for justification that left him shouting his grief and rage into emptiness that offered no echo.

The paramedics forced him onto a gurney with

practiced efficiency, strapping his burned limbs down with restraints to prevent further injury to himself or others. His body was alive, damaged but functional enough to face trial and prison. But his mind was already ash, trapped forever in the night his daughter died screaming his name while flames consumed her. He hadn't perished in the fires he'd set, hadn't achieved the dramatic martyr's death he might have craved. Instead, he'd been dragged back into the world he tried to burn, broken and scarred and consumed by grief that would never heal.

Shea watched as the ambulance doors slammed shut on Gary Richardson's ravaged face and manic laughter. Her jaw tightened as the vehicle pulled away, its sirens silent because there was no emergency anymore. Just the slow, inevitable processing of justice. This didn't feel like victory.

~

Days later, Shea stood alone in the county jail's stark corridor, staring through a small, reinforced window set into the heavy metal door of Richardson's cell. He sat on the concrete bench with his bandaged arms trembling, rocking slowly back and forth in a motion that suggested his mind had retreated somewhere law enforcement couldn't follow.

The burns on his arms and face were beginning the slow process of healing, though the scars would mark him for life. The doctors said he'd been incredibly lucky, or unlucky, depending on perspective, to escape with injuries that weren't life-threatening. He would live to stand trial, to face the families whose homes he'd destroyed and the memory of Tommy Garrett, the homeless man he'd deliberately murdered.

His voice came out as a harsh rasp when he noticed her watching through the window. "Now you know." A bitter smile curled across his burned lips like a wound reopening. "Now you all know exactly how it feels to lose Christmas forever. To have the season poisoned with memories of fire and death."

She stared at him for a long, silent beat, her expression unreadable behind the professional mask she'd perfected . Then, she turned deliberately and walked down the corridor without speaking a single word, leaving his hollow pronouncement to echo against the cinder block walls of his cage where it would die unheard.

~

But Misty Hollow didn't lose Christmas, despite Richardson's best efforts to steal it from them.

In the days following the destruction of St. Mary's fellowship hall, something remarkable happened. The people rallied with a determination that surprised even those who'd lived in the close-knit community their entire lives. Neighbors appeared at each other's doors carrying boxes filled with toys and warm winter coats for children whose families had lost everything. Local bakers worked overtime to donate thousands of cookies and treats. Seamstresses gathered in living rooms to stitch new ornaments from donated fabric. Fathers and sons drove to nearby tree farms, purchasing and cutting fresh spruce trees to replace those destroyed or feared contaminated by Richardson's accelerants.

Where paralyzing fear had smothered them just weeks ago, watching their traditions burn one by one, resolve now burned steadier and brighter than any destructive fire ever could. The community had stared into the darkness of one man's grief-fueled rage and decided collectively that they would not surrender their joy to his pain.

The elementary school organized a massive ornament-making drive, with every child in grades K-6 creating handmade decorations from construction paper, popsicle sticks, and glitter. The high school choir volunteered to perform at an outdoor ceremony despite the brutal December cold. Local businesses pooled resources to purchase new lights and decorations. Even families who typically kept Christmas celebrations private and modest contributed what they could to the communal effort.

On Christmas Eve, as darkness fell early over the mountain town, the entire community gathered in the town square. Snowflakes drifted down from heavy clouds like soft ash, the air sharp with the scent of fresh pine and the warm vanilla smell of melting candle wax. Instead of elaborate decorations, every person who attended carried a single white candle, creating a sea of small flames that swayed and flickered in the hush of the winter night.

In the center of the square stood a spruce tree much smaller than the massive specimen that had dominated previous ceremonies. Perhaps ten feet tall instead of forty, hastily decorated with the mismatched ribbons and borrowed ornaments that generous neighbors had contributed. It was imperfect, humble in its simplicity, and somehow more beautiful because of what it represented: resilience in the face of destruction, community overcoming individual tragedy, hope refusing to be extinguished.

Mayor Ferguson stepped onto the small platform that had been erected that afternoon. His voice cracked with genuine emotion as he addressed the crowd. "Fire tried to take our traditions from us. One man's grief nearly succeeded in destroying what generations of our families built together. But tonight, standing here in the cold with all of you, we show that light always returns. Darkness cannot prevail when people choose to stand together."

One by one, children from the elementary school stepped forward with ceremonial dignity far beyond their years, carefully plugging in strands of donated light bulbs that had been woven through the modest tree's branches. The tree flickered uncertainly for a moment, a brief darkness that made everyone hold their breath, then blazed to life in warm golden tones against the pristine white snow.

A murmur of relief and wonder spread through

the assembled crowd like ripples on a pond, then lifted and transformed into song. Soft carols at first, voices tentative and rough with emotion, but gradually growing stronger as confidence returned. The music carried on the night air like a promise made and kept, like a declaration that beauty and tradition could survive even the most determined assault.

"Silent Night" gave way to "O Holy Night," then "Hark the Herald Angels Sing" as the impromptu choir found its voice. Children's voices mixed with their parents', elderly residents harmonizing with teenagers, the entire community creating something that transcended individual grief and fear.

At the edge of the town square, partially hidden in shadows away from the central gathering, Shea stood beside Trevor. Her right hand throbbed with steady, insistent pain beneath its clean white bandages. But for the first time since the fires began weeks ago, she found herself able to breathe deeply without her chest constricting with anxiety. She looked away from the bulge under Trevor's jacket where he wore a thick bandage of his own.

The warm light reflecting off the snow illuminated his face, and it was not the angry orange of destructive fire. It was the gentle golden glow of hope, resilience, and community refusing to surrender to darkness.

Trevor leaned close to her, his voice still rough and damaged from smoke inhalation but carrying unmistakable warmth. "Beautiful, isn't it? All this light outshines his flames completely."

Shea's lips curved into the first genuine smile she'd managed in what felt like months. "Hope always does, Trevor. Always."

Their shoulders brushed together as they stood watching the ceremony, neither pulling away from the contact. The moment held weight and meaning beyond words. Two people who'd fought through fire and chaos together, finding something solid to hold onto in the aftermath. For once, Shea let herself fully exhale, feeling the crushing weight of responsibility slide from her chest. It wouldn't disappear entirely. She was still the sheriff, still responsible for protecting these people. But for tonight, she could share that burden.

Around them, the town hummed with a resilience that went deeper than mere survival. They were scarred but unbroken, marked by trauma but not defined by it. Misty Hollow had stared into the abyss of one man's destructive grief and chosen to respond with light instead of darkness, with community instead of fear, with hope instead of despair.

The town square glowed steady and bright in the falling snow, the modest tree shining with a light that felt warmer and more meaningful than any elaborate display from previous years. Hundreds of individual candles were held high by both young and old hands, creating a constellation of hope that pushed back against the winter darkness.

Light outshone the flames that had tried to consume them.

As carols filled the cold December air and snow continued falling, Shea finally allowed herself to believe that Misty Hollow's Christmas had survived. Scarred, certainly. Changed forever, absolutely. But survived, nevertheless.

And that was enough.

Chapter Twelve

The town square ceremony had ended hours ago, and most families had returned to their homes to continue private celebrations surrounded by people they loved.

Shea stood in her living room, staring at the unlit Christmas tree that she and Trevor had decorated together what felt like a lifetime ago. The spruce still stood in the corner where they'd placed it, adorned with mismatched ornaments and the wooden stars his mother had carved. It had remained dark since that night—a beautiful ghost waiting for permission to come alive.

Heidi dozed contentedly on her bed by the fireplace, worn out from the day's excitement and the long ceremony in the town square. The German Shepherd's presence was comforting, a reminder that some things remained constant even when the world felt like it was burning down.

A knock at the door made Shea's heart skip

unexpectedly. She knew who it would be. Trevor had texted an hour ago asking if he could stop by with "something important." She'd changed out of her uniform into comfortable jeans and a soft burgundy sweater, then immediately second-guessed the decision. Why did it suddenly feel like a first date rather than her partner dropping by after a long case?

When she opened the door, Trevor stood on her porch with snowflakes catching in his dark hair and a canvas bag slung over his shoulder. He'd also changed from his uniform into civilian clothes. Dark jeans and a gray Henley that made his eyes look more blue than usual. His smile was warm but carried an edge of nervousness she rarely saw from him.

"Merry Christmas Eve," he said, stomping snow from his boots before entering. "I hope I'm not intruding on your quiet time."

"You're never an intrusion." She meant it more than she'd intended to reveal. "Come in before you freeze."

Trevor set the bag down carefully near the tree, and Shea caught a glimpse of wrapped packages inside. "I brought a few things," he said, pulling off his winter coat. "Figured we earned the right to actually celebrate after everything."

"We did." She took his coat and hung it by the door. "Can I get you something to drink? I have wine, coffee, hot chocolate..."

"Wine sounds perfect." He moved toward the tree,

studying it the way someone might examine a painting in a museum. "It's still beautiful, even without the lights."

Shea disappeared into the kitchen and returned with two glasses of red wine and a bottle she'd been saving for a special occasion that never seemed to arrive. Tonight felt special enough. When she handed Trevor his glass, their fingers brushed, and neither pulled away immediately from the contact.

"I've been thinking." She set her glass on the coffee table. "About what you said that night we decorated this tree. About not using the lights."

Trevor watched her carefully, his expression open and patient. "You said you weren't ready. I understood."

"I think I'm ready now." She moved to the tree and crouched beside the outlet where the cord still waited, untouched since that night. "Richardson tried to make us afraid of light, of joy, of Christmas itself. But I watched the town tonight, hundreds of people holding candles, refusing to let his darkness win…" She looked up at Trevor. "I don't want to give him that power over my own home."

"Then don't," Trevor said simply. "Light it up, Shea."

She plugged in the cord, and the tree blazed to life in warm golden tones that filled her living room with a glow that felt like hope made visible. The mismatched ornaments caught and reflected the light, creating patterns on the walls that danced with gentle beauty. It wasn't the elaborate display that had dominated St. Mary's fellowship hall. It was better, because it was real and hard-won and theirs.

Shea stood slowly, surprised by the emotion tightening her throat. "It's perfect."

"It really is." Trevor looked at her rather than the tree.

They stood together in the soft light, the moment stretching into something that felt significant beyond words. Finally, Trevor cleared his throat and gestured toward the bag he'd brought. "So, I have some things for you. Nothing fancy, but..."

"Trevor, you didn't have to get me anything."

"I know. I wanted to." He pulled out a wrapped package and handed it to her with an expression that mixed hope and vulnerability. "This one first."

She settled onto the couch and carefully unwrapped the package, taking care not to tear the paper decorated with silver snowflakes. Inside was a leather journal, its cover soft and well-made, with her initials embossed on the front in gold lettering.

"I know you keep case notes." He sat beside her. "But I thought maybe you'd want something for other things too. Thoughts, feelings, observations that aren't about work. A place that's just yours."

She ran her fingers over the smooth leather, touched by the thoughtfulness behind the gift. "This is beautiful, Trevor. Thank you."

"There's more." He handed her a second, smaller package.

This one contained a delicate silver bracelet with a single charm—a small compass rose. Shea held it up to the light, watching it catch and reflect the glow from the tree.

"You're someone who always finds her way," Trevor said quietly. "Even when the path isn't clear, even when everything's on fire, you orient yourself and move forward. I wanted you to have something that reminded you of that strength when things get difficult."

Tears threatened and she blinked them back. "I don't know what to say. These are incredibly thoughtful."

"You don't have to say anything." He took a sip of his wine, then added, "Actually, there's one more thing, but it's not wrapped."

He reached into the bag and pulled out a framed photograph that made Shea's breath catch. It was from the town square ceremony earlier that evening. She hadn't even noticed anyone photographing them. The image captured the two of them standing at the edge of the crowd, illuminated by candlelight, their shoulders touching as they watched the community come together. The expression on both their faces was soft, unguarded, and spoke of something deeper than professional partnership.

"Lucy's husband took this," Trevor explained. "He

sent it to me and said we should have a copy. I had it printed at the pharmacy while they were still open."

"It's perfect." She stared at the photograph. "It captures everything about tonight."

She set the frame carefully on the coffee table and turned to Trevor with determination. "Now it's my turn. Stay here."

She disappeared into her bedroom and returned with two packages wrapped in simple brown paper tied with twine. Humble compared to Trevor's silver snowflake paper, but wrapped with care nonetheless.

"I wasn't sure when I'd have the courage to give you these." She handed him the first package. "But tonight feels right."

Trevor unwrapped it to find a vintage compass, brass and beautifully preserved, in a leather case. The compass had clearly been made decades ago, its face showing slight age but still perfectly functional.

"It belonged to my father," Shea explained, her voice carrying the weight of memory. "He was a sheriff too, in a small town in Montana before he passed away when I was in college. He used to say that law enforcement was about finding true north even when everyone around you pointed in different directions."

Trevor's hands were gentle as he held the compass, understanding the significance of the gift. "I can't accept this. It's too important."

"You can, and you will," she said firmly. "You've been my true north these past few weeks, Trevor. When

I was drowning in pressure and doubt, you kept me grounded and focused. I want you to have it."

He set the compass carefully beside his wine glass and pulled her into a hug that lasted longer than professional partners typically embraced. When they separated, both pretended not to notice the slight moisture in the other's eyes.

"There's one more." She handed him the second package.

This one was softer, and Trevor's expression grew puzzled as he unwrapped it. Inside was a hand-knitted scarf in deep navy blue, clearly made with skill but also obvious love in every stitch.

"You knit?" Trevor asked with genuine surprise.

"My grandmother taught me when I was young. I haven't done it in years, but after we decorated the tree that night, I couldn't sleep, so I started this." She gestured at the scarf. "It gave me something productive to do with my hands when my mind was too wired to rest. I thought about you with every row—about your steadiness, your humor, the way you've had my back through everything. From my first day in Misty Hollow."

Trevor wrapped the scarf around his neck immediately, despite being indoors and warm. "I'm never taking this off."

"You'll have to eventually," She laughed. "But I'm glad you like it."

They sat in comfortable silence for a moment,

sipping their wine and watching the tree lights dance. Heidi had woken up and wandered over, resting her head on Shea's knee as if to remind them she was still part of this family.

"We should toast." Trevor lifted his glass. "To surviving the worst and finding light on the other side."

"To partnership." She touched her glass to his with a soft clink. "Both professional and..." she hesitated, then took the leap, "...and personal."

Trevor's eyes held hers over the rim of his glass. "I was hoping you'd say that."

They drank, then set their glasses down. The moment stretched between them, heavy with unspoken words and feelings that had been building since long before the fires started.

"Trevor," Shea began, then stopped, unsure how to articulate what she was feeling.

"I know," he said softly. "I feel it too."

"This is complicated. We work together. There are rules about fraternization—"

"Shea." Trevor took her bandaged hand gently in his. "I'm not asking for anything to happen tonight or tomorrow or even next week. I'm just asking you to know, to be certain, that what I feel for you goes beyond professional respect or partnership. You're extraordinary. Not just as a sheriff, but as a person."

"You make me want to be braver than I am," Shea confessed, her voice barely above a whisper. "When I'm with you, I feel like I can handle anything. Like the weight isn't quite so crushing."

"That's because you were never meant to carry it alone." His thumb traced gentle circles on the back of her hand. "I'm here, Shea. For the fires and the quiet moments. For the victories and the failures. For all of it."

"That's terrifying," she admitted with a shaky laugh.

"I know. But the best things usually are."

They sat close together on the couch, the tree glowing beside them and Heidi curled at their feet. The wine warmed them from the inside while the fireplace crackled softly, creating a cocoon of safety and peace after weeks of constant vigilance.

Shea leaned against Trevor's shoulder, testing the gesture, and felt his arm come around her in response. Solid, warm, and reassuring. She'd spent so long being strong, being the one who protected everyone else, that the simple act of accepting support felt revolutionary.

"Tell me something about yourself that I don't know," she murmured, her eyes growing heavy with the exhaustion of finally being able to relax.

"I'm terrible at ice skating," Trevor said, a smile in his voice. "Absolutely awful. I fall down constantly and look like a newborn giraffe trying to stand up."

"That's oddly comforting to know." She laughed softly. "I'm scared of spiders. Absolutely terrified. Which is ridiculous for someone who faces down armed suspects without flinching."

"Everyone's afraid of something. It makes us human."

They continued trading small revelations—favorite foods, childhood embarrassments, dreams they'd given up and dreams they still held secretly. The conversation meandered naturally, neither forced nor awkward, with comfortable silences punctuating the words.

At some point, Shea's eyes drifted closed, her head resting more heavily against Trevor's shoulder. His voice grew quieter, transitioning from conversation to gentle murmuring that sounded almost like a lullaby without words.

"Sleep," he said softly. "You're safe here."

And for the first time in weeks, She believed it completely. The fires were over. Gary Richardson was behind bars. The community was healing. And she wasn't alone anymore. Not in her work, not in her fears, and not in the possibility of something beautiful growing from the ashes of trauma.

Trevor's breathing eventually slowed and deepened as well, his head resting against the top of hers. The wine glasses sat empty on the coffee table. The tree continued its gentle glow. Heidi sighed contentedly in her sleep.

Outside, snow fell softly over Misty Hollow, blanketing the town in pristine white that covered the scars of recent fires. Christmas Eve settled over the community like a benediction. Not perfect, not unmarked by tragedy, but precious nonetheless.

In Shea's living room, two people who had fought through darkness together found peace in each other's presence, sleeping side by side on a couch beneath the warm glow of a Christmas tree that had waited patiently to shine.

Light had outshone the flames.

And love, hesitant, complicated, but undeniably real, began to bloom in the space where fear had once taken root.

Tomorrow would bring Christmas morning, new challenges, and the ongoing work of healing a traumatized community. But tonight, on Christmas Eve, there was only this: two souls finding comfort and hope in each other, surrounded by thoughtful gifts and the gentle promise of something beautiful yet to come.

The tree's lights reflected off the compass and the photograph, the journal and the scarf. All tokens of understanding and affection that spoke louder than any declaration.

And in the quiet of that holy night, Misty Hollow's Christmas was finally, truly, complete.

Dear Reader,

157

My all your Christmases be filled with light and hope. If you liked this book, please leave a review or a rating on Amazon. Reviews are the lifeblood of authors.

158

www.cynthiahickey.com
Cynthia Hickey is a multi-published and best-selling author of cozy mysteries and romantic suspense/thrillers. She has taught writing at many conferences and small writing retreats. She and her husband run the publishing press, Winged Publications. They live in Arizona and Arkansas, becoming snowbirds with three dogs. They have ten grandchildren who keep them busy and tell everyone they know that "Nana is a writer."

Connect with me on FaceBook
Twitter
Sign up for my newsletter and receive a free short story

www.cynthiahickey.com

Follow me on Amazon
And Bookbub
Shop my bookstore on my website for better prices and autographed books.

Enjoy other books by Cynthia Hickey

Romantic Suspense and Thrillers

The Sheriff of Misty Hollow
Girls' Weekend Survival
The Threat

Evil Returns
Drowned in Silence
Banner of Death

Cowboys of Misty Hollow
Cowboy Jeopardy
Cowboy Peril
Cowboy Hazard
Cowgirl Blaze
Cowboy Uncertainty
Cowboy Christmas Crisis
Cowboy Pitfall
Snowed in For Christmas With a Cowboy

Stay on the Ranch with the whole set

Misty Hollow
Secrets of Misty Hollow
Deceptive Peace
Calm Surface
Lightning Never Strikes Twice
Lethal Inheritance
Bitter Isolation
Say I Don't
Christmas Stalker
Bridge to Safety
When Night Falls
A Place to Hide
Mountain Refuge

Stay in Misty Hollow for a while. Get the entire series here!

Secrets of the South
The Lovers' Lane Murders
The Prom Night Hitchhiker

The Seven Deadly Sins series
Deadly Pride
Deadly Covet
Deadly Lust
Deadly Glutton
Deadly Envy
Deadly Sloth
Deadly Anger
Get the whole set here

Brothers Steele
Sharp as Steele
Carved in Steele
Forged in Steele
Brothers Steele (All three in one)

The Brothers of Copper Pass
Wyatt's Warrant
Dirk's Defense
Stetson's Secret
Houston's Hope
Dallas's Dare
Seth's Sacrifice

Malcolm's Misunderstanding
The Brothers of Copper Pass Boxed Set

Highland Springs

Murder Live
Say Bye to Mommy
To Breathe Again
Highland Springs Murders (all 3 in one)

Colors of Evil Series

Shades of Crimson
Coral Shadows
Indigo Nightmares

The Pretty Must Die Series

Ripped in Red, book 1
Pierced in Pink, book 2
Wounded in White, book 3
Worthy, The Complete Story

Lisa Paxton Mystery Series

Eenie Meenie Miny Mo
Jack Be Nimble
Hickory Dickory Dock
Boxed Set

Hearts of Courage
A Heart of Valor
The Game
Suspicious Minds
After the Storm
Local Betrayal
Hearts of Courage Boxed Set

Overcoming Evil series
Mistaken Assassin
Captured Innocence
Mountain of Fear
Exposure at Sea
A Secret to Die for
Collision Course
Romantic Suspense of 5 books in 1

Wife for Hire – Private Investigators
Saving Sarah
Lesson for Lacey
Mission for Meghan
Long Way for Lainie
Aimed at Amy
Wife for Hire (all five in one)

One Hour (A short story thriller)

COZY MYSTERIES

The Tail Waggin' Mysteries
Cat-Eyed Witness
The Dog Who Found a Body
Troublesome Twosome
Four-Legged Suspect
Unwanted Christmas Guest
Wedding Day Cat Burglar
The entire Tail Waggin' Series

Tiny House Mysteries
No Small Caper
Caper Goes Missing
Caper Finds a Clue
Caper's Dark Adventure
A Strange Game for Caper
Caper Steals Christmas
Caper Finds a Treasure
Tiny House Mysteries boxed set

A Hollywood Murder
Killer Pose, book 1
Killer Snapshot, book 2
Shoot to Kill, book 3
Kodak Kill Shot, book 4
To Snap a Killer
Hollywood Murder Mysteries

Shady Acres Mysteries

Beware the Orchids
Path to Nowhere
Poison Foliage
Poinsettia Madness
Deadly Greenhouse Gases
Vine Entrapment
Shady Acres Boxed Set

Nosy Neighbor Series
Anything For A Mystery
A Killer Plot
Skin Care Can Be Murder
Death By Baking
Jogging Is Bad For Your Health
Poison Bubbles
A Good Party Can Kill You
Nosy Neighbor collection

Christmas with Stormi Nelson

The Summer Meadows Series
Fudge-Laced Felonies
Candy-Coated Secrets
Chocolate-Covered Crime
Maui Macadamia Madness
All four novels in one collection

The River Valley Mystery Series
Deadly Neighbors

Advance Notice
The Librarian's Last Chapter
All three novels in one collection

Cozies not part of a series
Coffee, Tea, or Murder
Scones to Die For
Mischief and Mayhem

Time Travel
The Portal

Historical cozy
Hazel's Quest

Historical Romances
Novellas
Runaway Sue
Taming the Sheriff
Sweet Apple Blossom
A Doctor's Agreement
A Lady Maid's Honor
A Touch of Sugar
Love Over Par
Heart of the Emerald
A Sketch of Gold
Her Lonely Heart
Abigail's Proposal

Sophia's Hope
Moira's Quest
Savannah's Trial
Josephine's Dream
A Most Reluctant Bride
Competing Hearts
A Teacher's Heart
Lesson of Love

SERIES
Finding Love the Harvey Girl Way
Cooking With Love
Guiding With Love
Serving With Love
Warring With Love
All 4 in 1

Finding Love in Disaster
The Rancher's Dilemma
The Teacher's Rescue
The Soldier's Redemption

Woman of courage Series

A Love For Delicious
Ruth's Redemption
Charity's Gold Rush
Mountain Redemption
They Call Her Mrs. Sheriff

Woman of Courage series

Short Story Westerns
Flowers of the Desert

Contemporary

Romance in Paradise
Maui Magic
Sunset Kisses
Deep Sea Love
3 in 1

The Red Hat's Club (Contemporary novellas)

Finally
Suddenly
Surprisingly
The Red Hat's Club 3 – in 1

STANDALONES
Finding a Way Home
Service of Love
Hillbilly Cinderella
Unraveling Love
I'd Rather Kiss My Horse

Whisper Sweet Nothings (a Valentine short romance)

Christmas Romances (Contemporary and Historical)
Dear Jillian
Romancing the Fabulous Cooper Brothers
Handcarved Christmas
The Payback Bride
Curtain Calls and Christmas Wishes
Christmas Gold
A Christmas Stamp
Snowflake Kisses
Merry's Secret Santa
Holly's Hope
A Christmas Deception
A Christmas Castle